Miracles

Miracles

HEAVEN IS AT MY CEILING

JOHN J. SEIDEN

CITIOFBOOKS, INC.
3736 Eubank NE Suite A1
Albuquerque, NM 87111-3579
www.citiofbooks.com

Hotline: 1 (877) 389-2759
Fax: 1 (505) 930-7244

Ordering Information:
Quantity sales. Special discounts are available on quantity purchases by corporations, associations, and others. For details, contact the publisher at the address above.

Printed in the United States of America.

ISBN-13:   Paperback   979-8-89391-033-9
                   eBook   979-8-89391-034-6

Library of Congress Control Number: 2024906146

Introduction

This book is about my life experiences with direct contact between God, His angels and ghosts. Everything in this book is real; nothing has been embellished or invented. The existence of God, His angels and ghosts are explained during numerous encounters with physical and visual contact. I have been all over the world both with the U.S. Government and with my private business and I have experienced numerous forms of contact in many countries. Each form of contact has served to reinforce my love for God and his angels and to respect the appearance of ghosts as well.

With my photographic memory, I am able to remember occurrences from the time I was a young child to the present. I feel extremely blessed to have had such holy experiences over the years and consider them to be true miracles. I know that God and His angels would be happy that I am able to fully recollect all of my holy experiences and relate them to everyone interested in His existence and that of His angels. I really don't know how many other individuals have had such contact with God and his angels. However, I consider it a privilege to have had such contact over the years and look forward to more such contacts in the future.

I grew up in Seattle, Washington. My father was employed with the Seattle Post Intelligencer Newspaper and studied at the University of Washington where he obtained his Master of Arts degree. I went to elementary school in Seattle, walking about a mile to school every day by myself. My parents enrolled both my brother and myself in a swimming class when I was 6 and my brother was 8. We both learned to swim at our young age in a regulation size swimming pool. In order to graduate from our swimming class, we had to swim all around the circumference of the pool. It was difficult, but we both accomplished the exercise and graduated accordingly!

In the late 1940's, it was safe for a young child to walk to school alone. I remember my kindergarten teacher, Mrs. Riley. My friends and I used to become rowdy at times and Mrs. Riley had a wooden ruler which she hit the undersides of our wrists to punish us. It was really painful and we behaved quickly! We soon learned that it was not appropriate to act up by running around the classroom. This learning period stuck in my memory for many years and I quickly learned to respect the teacher along with other forms of authority in life. Ignoring authority, whether in a classroom or elsewhere, is only grounds for punishment!

One of our neighbors had a cherry tree next to our home. I loved cherries and borrowed a ladder to climb up and pick some cherries. Nothing is more delicious than eating fresh cherries! Another neighbor used to make fresh blackberry pies using the blackberry bushes growing behind her home. Every time she baked the blackberry pies, the aroma was all over her home and I could smell the pies outside her home as well. This may have been the reason I began my interest in baking due to the blackberry pies. One of my best friends lived in the house and I was always happy to visit him in the hope that I could have a piece of the delicious pie!

We lived in Tacoma Washington for several years before moving to Seattle. I remember my parents growing several fig trees in front of our house. Nothing is better than eating fresh figs off the tree! The figs were so delicious and the skin was soft as well. It reminds me of the fig newton cookie which was my favorite cookie when I was growing up. My parents had a vegetable garden in front of our home and my mother planted various vegetables in the garden and spent a great deal of time taking care of the vegetables. This may have sparked my interest in growing vegetables later in life due to my mother's interest in gardening!

I grew up in an Army family since my father was an Army officer. I was born in Springfield, Ohio, when my father was assigned to Wright Patterson Air Force Base. He was in the Army Air Corps on active duty. He was soon assigned to Bremerhaven, Germany and we all went as a family, my father, mother, brother and me. The year was 1949 and I was only six years old. We went by ship to Germany and it took about two weeks to arrive. Everyone on board got seasick and we all had to wear life jackets during safety drills outside on deck and sucked on lemons to keep from getting any sicker.

I remember dishes sliding off the tables in the dining room when the ship moved from side to side. I even remember walking up and down the stairs below to our room, holding onto the railing for dear life to avoid falling down. As I remember, it took a week or more to travel from New York to Germany aboard the ship. It actually felt like an eternity since the ship moved so slowly. When having a meal in the dining room, from time to time an individual would run outdoors to the deck and rush to the railing, becoming seasick. This would happen time and time again since the ship was rocking back and forth on occasion, producing nausea for anyone eating a meal.

We were transplanted into the U.S. Army Occupation of Germany after the war ended. Everywhere we looked was scenes of bombed out buildings in piles of bricks. It was difficult to believe how the Germans could have survived all of the bombing. I specifically remember walking down the sidewalk with my family, seeing signs of total devastation. Even though I was only six years old, I felt sad for the people of Germany. How anyone could live after such a pounding during the war was simply incomprehensible. Block after block, everything was in a shambles with very few buildings left intact.

We were living in a large beautiful house that was previously owned by a German Colonel. The house was very spacious with a large, marble bathroom. I remember the beautiful, marble bathtub. I have never seen such a bathtub before and was simply awestruck! It was as if we were living in a mansion which was elegantly furnished. The home had numerous bedrooms which were immaculately furnished. It appeared that the previous occupants just simply vanished, leaving everything in its place. We were very lucky to have such a large, wonderful home to stay in during my father's tour of duty.

We had a boxer dog named Tina. We used to play with Tina in our backyard all of the time. Tina was a female with very strong muscles, as most boxers have. She used to drool all of the time which is characteristic of boxers. One morning, when I got up, I put my foot down into a very large moist pile of poop which Tina had thoughtfully placed next to my bed. This was somewhat unnerving, to say the least! That was quite a wakeup call! Of course, Tina, being a dog could not be blamed for this transgression. I never forgot this canine encounter and hope that I never experience it again!

We had a nanny named Hanna. She was very pretty and took care of my brother and myself all of the time. This was my first experience with someone from Germany and I was very happy to be with her. Since my father spoke German, he had no problem communicating with Hanna. As a matter of fact, my father spoke five languages including German, Russian, Portuguese, French and Spanish. My parents wanted to bring Hanna to the U.S. when we returned but she had developed tuberculosis and was not eligible to come with us. We were all so sad when we had to leave Hanna in Germany since she was part of the family and simply delightful to be with!

The water was not safe to drink in Germany since the water pipes were damaged due to the war. Therefore, we had to drink coffee which was made with boiled water. I really didn't like the taste of coffee, being only six, but had no choice. I remember sitting at the dinner table and sipping the hot coffee. It was really quite a challenge for someone so young as myself. To me, coffee had a very weird taste, something I had never previously experienced. Now, I love coffee and I even grind my own coffee beans. I even add sweetened condensed milk to make a perfect cup and, "low calorie", to boot! Now, scientists are saying that coffee is very good for you and increases your life expectancy with from one to three cups per day.

One day, my father heard noises outside our house near the garbage cans. He went outside and found two German children going through the garbage cans to find food since they were starving. My father brought them into our house to have dinner with us. We were all delighted at having the children join us since there was little food available due to the war. I felt very proud of my father due to his sincerity and compassion for the children. The children were no older than nine or ten years old and were very polite at the dinner table. They enjoyed eating with us and we enjoyed their company as well.

My father had bought riding boots for my brother and myself. They were beautiful brown leather boots and I always enjoyed wearing them. My father was a mounted cavalry officer in the Army and always liked to ride horses with his riding boots. My brother and I both rode horses at a young age for a short ride only. Being in the saddle so young was scary since the horse was so large to us. On one occasion, my father discovered that my saddle was not tightened securely and admonished the owner of the horse riding stable accordingly since I might have slipped off the horse accidentally and injured myself.

One thing which I clearly remember is my father's buying Hohner harmonicas and hand accordions which my brother and I played. One of the harmonica had a push button on its end which regulated the notes and the other harmonica had a long toggle button which you had to press to activate. The musical instruments are part of the German culture and were very enjoyable playing. My father also bought us hand accordions which were a lot of fun playing. The accordions were pretty small, measuring about eight inches long and six inches wide. They had buttons on the instrument which you had to press to play different notes. There were also straps on both sides which fit around each hand.

I also remember going to the store and buying licorice pipes with red centers which depicted a lit pipe. I developed my craving for licorice at that time and still love the candy. I think that licorice made in Germany is perhaps among the best licorice that you can find anywhere. Speaking of pipes, my father used to smoke a German pipe which was made of a woven material with a meerschaum bowl at the end. The meerschaum was made of a claylike material which cooled the smoke and gave it a sweet taste as well. When I was in college, I had bought a meerschaum pipe at the local tobacco store and enjoyed the sweet, cool smoke as well. My college classmates in my dormitory like to smoke pipes as well and I even gave smoking classes to them to teach how to smoke pipes!

I also have fond memories of traveling to the Black Forest in Bad Mergentheim. I specifically remember the beautiful black walnut trees in full bloom across the gorgeous meadows. The meadows seemed to go on forever since I could never see the end. I remember picking up black walnuts on the ground and was amazed at the size of the shell. The shells were so large and hard that I did not see how they could be opened. My father told me that you would have to use a hammer to open the shells. One day, while driving in the Black Forest, my father had to ask for directions during a family excursion since he was not familiar with the location; but we made it finally to our destination!

I also remember my father going on a rabbit hunt with some of his Army friends using a shotgun. He brought back rabbits to our home which were cooked and tasted really good! I had never tasted rabbit before but had a lucky rabbit's foot with me. I was a little nervous at the time about eating rabbit but since my mother had done the cooking, I decided to go ahead and, "take the plunge". The rabbit had a very good taste, as I remember, but a little on the wild side since it was a game food. I also remember biting down on buckshot from time to time but it wasn't that bad as long as you spit out the buckshot!

While in school in the first grade, I remember studying the German language. "Ist das ein strassenbahn? Ja, das ist ein strassenbahn!" Studying a foreign language at the young age of six seemed somewhat strange to me. Everyone in my class was an American with parents who were in the military. Therefore, I felt somewhat comforted at learning a foreign language with other children my own age. I later studied German for two years in college at Purdue University. I also studied French in high school for two years. In addition, I studied Korean in South Korea while I was working as an Army officer and with the U.S. Government for five years. I think that my studying German in Germany at a young age helped prepare me to study other languages in the future.

While in Germany, we rode a school bus to school manned by U.S. Army MP's since we were living there under the U.S. Army of Occupation in 1949. I felt somewhat uncomfortable traveling with MP's to school but my father told me that they were there for our own protection so I never questioned their presence. There was always one MP on the bus at all times for security. This was my first close contact with an MP since I had never seen one so near before. Later in life when I joined the Army, I had contact with MP's when I entered military bases. Being an officer, the MP's always saluted me as part of standard Army protocol.

While in Germany, we went on a package tour to France, Holland and Belgium. I remember the Eiffel Tower and the Arc de Triumph. I had the distinct privilege of having to go to the bathroom in the base of the Arc de Triumph where several bathrooms were located! I wonder how many other individuals had the opportunity to use the bathroom at the base of the Arc de Triumph, let alone know it was there. We went on a glass-bottomed boat in the canals of Holland and I distinctly remember the windmills and tulip fields; a beautiful and colorful sight indeed. In Belgium, I enjoyed the chocolate pudding at one of their restaurants and know now that the Belgians excel in chocolate such as Godiva. I also remember the excellent bread in Europe, brown and crispy on the outside and soft and delicate on the inside.

Leaving Germany again was by ship and this time, both my brother and myself caught the measles. This was a very unnerving episode since we were both quarantined in the medical section of the ship until we arrived back in the U.S. I was really nervous to be quarantined in the medical section of the ship since I did not fully realize that measles are highly contagious. When we arrived back in the U.S., we were taken by separate ambulances to an Army hospital for further treatment. The ambulance ride seemed to be unnecessary to me at the time but I was in no position to question the decision since I was only six years old and was scared.

We returned to the United States in 1950 and settled briefly in Palo Alto, California. I remember walking to school beside a farmland and looking at the mountains all around. Quite a beautiful sight! I even remember "borrowing" a few carrots from the farmer's carrot crop a few times while on the way home from school. I don't think that the farmer ever missed the carrots but never asked him anyway since he was never outside when I walked home. The carrots were simply delicious! Later in life, I would grow my own carrots in my back yard along with ruby red loose leaf lettuce, snap peas, tomatoes, strawberries and cucumbers. There is nothing better than growing your own vegetables since they are fresher than those which you can buy in the grocery stores and better tasting.

We soon moved to Tacoma, Washington and later to Seattle. My father obtained his MA at the University of Washington. I remember living in Seattle in two different homes. In one home, I had to keep my bike downstairs for security. One day, I was bringing my bike upstairs and was almost at the top when I fell all the way to the bottom with my bike on top of me. The bike was heavy, having been made in Germany. There was only one gear and a bell that had to be rung with your thumb. I really didn't know what had happened, being somewhat stunned at falling all the way down to the bottom of the stairs. At the time, I couldn't believe that I was not hurt from the fall. I didn't tell my father since I didn't want to get into trouble. At the time, I was unaware of my guardian Angel who would always be with me for protection.

On another occasion, I was riding my bike with some of my friends and I wanted to show off by riding the bike with no hands which kids sometimes do. Suddenly, the bike locked up in the middle of the street with several oncoming cars approaching. I was thrown over the handlebars and landed in the middle of the intersection. A driver of one of the oncoming cars stopped his car and got out to check on my condition. "Are you okay?" he asked. I replied, "Yes, I'm okay", somewhat shakily. He added, "Are you sure? You took quite a tumble". I replied, "I'm really fine. Just a few scrapes on my knee". I was really upset at my spill but happy that I had only sustained a few scrapes on my knee. At the time, I really didn't know how lucky I was to have avoided a serious injury and vowed henceforth to refrain from any additional risk taking. I never told my parents what had happened. I know now that my guardian Angel was also there to protect me from serious injury.I started my newspaper route in Seattle at the age of seven, delivering the Seattle Post Intelligencer newspaper. I used my bike to deliver the newspapers, going from house to house as is normally the case. I always gave the money I earned on my newspaper route to my father to help him pay bills. For the next ten years, I delivered newspapers in Seattle and later in Maryland from the age of seven to seventeen. I learned how to conduct my own business in this manner since I had to collect the money from the people on my newspaper route and give it to my newspaper manager. One of the best parts of delivering newspapers was during holidays when the customers on the route would give me a tip or gift. This was very enjoyable and much appreciated!

One of my cherished memories as a youth in Seattle was going fishing by myself. I only had to walk several blocks to fish for silver trout. I always managed to catch one when I went fishing. Both silver and rainbow trout were available but I never caught any rainbow trout, although I always wanted to catch one. The University of Washington was close by and I fished in a nearby stream. For bait, I had to dig in my back yard for worms. They were a little messy but the fish always loved to eat the worms, especially when they wriggled on the hook. I also caught grasshoppers as well to use for bait since they were also loved by the fish. They were a little difficult to put on the hook since they somehow knew that the end was near!

We moved to Maryland in 1952 when my father joined the CIA. I was only nine years old at the time and never even heard of Maryland. I do remember the noisy airplane ride, however, since it must have been a DC-3 propeller driven plane. The plane ride seemed like an eternity since it probably took seven or eight hours at the time. Before we boarded the plane, my brother and I were allowed to purchase some comic books and chewing gum. We even sang Frankie Laine's famous hit record, "High Noon", from the movie High Noon which starred Gary Cooper and Grace Kelly, in a duet before we boarded the plane. This is one of my fond memories of my brother and myself.

We settled in Wheaton, Maryland where I have lived for the rest of my life, except for overseas military, U.S. Government service and my own consulting business. I never knew where my father worked since working for the CIA at that time was a very clandestine activity. One day, while driving through Roselyn, Virginia, my father pointed out the building to me where he worked which was behind a barbed wire fence. The building appeared innocuous enough and I didn't question anything, being too young at the time to question anything. The CIA Headquarters is now located in Langley, Virginia; a fact widely known.

We lived in a rented house for several years before moving into an apartment. The house was very nice, located at the bottom of a steep hill. I remember during the winter time when there was snow all over the area that we used to go to sledding down the steep hill all the way to my home. Some of my friends had a toboggan which we all climbed on top of and roared down the hill together. This was a lot of fun and was the only time I had the pleasure of travelling on a toboggan down a snowy hill. I also remember roller skating down the sidewalk in front of my home and never even fell down! Since my father was in the Army, I used to put his helmet liner on my head and march down the sidewalk with a toy rifle on my shoulder, pretending to be in the Army. This was really a lot of fun!

We moved into an apartment in the early 50's on the third floor of the building At that time, there was no air conditioning and my father had installed window fans to keep cool in the summer. The only problem with living on the third floor of an apartment building was walking up three flights. I had a paper route at the time and did a lot of walking up the apartment floors in the adjoining apartments to deliver the newspapers. On Sunday morning I delivered the heaviest newspapers with the advertisements, magazines and comics inside. Luckily, there was a grocery store nearby and I, "borrowed" a shopping basket the night before and hid it to use to deliver the heavy Sunday newspapers. I even remember riding the shopping basket down some adjoining hills to save delivery time!

The year was 1954 and you could hear the rock and roll song, "Rock Around the Clock", by Bill Haley's Comets in someone's apartment. Suddenly, a large red meteor about 500 feet in diameter appeared overhead. The meteor made no noise but was rotating on its own axis and was moving from north to south. After about five to seven seconds, the meteor disappeared out of view. I was truly amazed at the sight and wondered if anyone else had seen the meteor. I never told this event to anyone at the time since I didn't know if I had witnessed the meteor alone or if anyone else had seen it. I never heard anything on the news about the meteor either on the day I saw it or on the following days. It may have been a premonition of things to come when I saw a red ball coming towards me before and after my grandfather died with three Angels appearing before me.

At about the same year, I was walking next to a shopping center adjacent to our apartment coming from a grocery store into a nearby alley. Suddenly, I was struck by a car driving down the alley and was knocked to the ground. The driver of the car got out to see whether I was injured. He asked me, "Are you okay? You had quite a spill!" I brushed myself off and told him, "I'm okay! I'm not hurt at all". I was happy that I was not hurt since I would have had to explain to my father what had happened and felt somewhat guilty at the time. Little did I know that my guardian Angel was taking care of me, preventing a serious injury from happening. At the time, I just felt lucky that I was not hurt!

We had moved to a new house in Wheaton, Maryland, soon thereafter. I always prayed during the evening every night between 2:00 a.m. and 4:00 a.m.:

"Now I lay me down to sleep,

I pray the Lord my soul to keep,

If I should die before I wake,

I pray the Lord my soul to take."

Suddenly, a strange light filled up the room. Since I didn't know what was causing the light, I went to my window and opened the blinds. When I opened the blinds, a bright, white star about four to five feet in diameter appeared. I was startled and continued to stare at the star for five to seven seconds before it disappeared. I simply could not believe my eyes. Why was a star appearing before me in the middle of the night? I didn't know the meaning of the star's appearance. I never told anyone about the star's appearance. I know now that the star was from God. No one else could have made a star appear before me in the middle of the night, especially after I was praying to God!

I attended Wheaton High School from 1955 to 1961. At that time, Wheaton High School was a Junior-Senior High School with grades from 7 to 12. I spent six years at Wheaton High School and truly enjoyed every year. While at Wheaton High School, I was fortunate to be inducted into the National Honor Society for both my Junior and Senior years. I was also inducted into the National Mathematics Society, Mu Alpha Theta, and the French National Honor Society. I was the best in my high school in speaking, reading and writing French. My teacher, Dr. Frey, used to have me stand in front of the blackboard and write sentences in French as he dictated them to me. I felt really honored to be able to perform in front of my class!

I was fascinated with organic gardening at the time and planted tomatoes, potatoes, grapes, raspberries and an assortment of flowers including roses, crocuses, ferns, daylilies, iris, dwarf marigolds, wax begonias and other plants and vegetables. I grew a large selection of sunflowers which were about ten inches in diameter.

These flowers were simply beautiful, having a very large interior and bright yellow flowers on their border. I even grew a number of castor bean plants which resembled palm trees. The plants were simply beautiful with large, green leaves and red stems. There were numerous castor beans inside each plant's pods which were poisonous, I later found out. Our dog, Von, once chewed a castor bean which had fallen to the ground and immediately gagged and spit the bean out, obviously realizing that it was not edible!

I bought a Venus flytrap plant and enjoyed feeding flies to the plant and watching the leaves close on its victim. Inside the leaves are hairs that trigger the leaves to close when an insect lands inside the leaves and brushes against the hairs. It's just like a science fiction movie, a little scary! I also bought several cactus plants which were simply beautiful with small yellow flowers in bloom from time to time. The cactus plants, however, had very sharp quills and really hurt if you happen to touch the plant by mistake. There are so many varieties of cactus plants with different shapes and sizes. They use very little water, of course, since the water is normally stored inside the plants, just like on the desert!

I managed my high school greenhouse for several years. While managing the greenhouse, I even grew tomato plants from seeds in seed flats. This was an especially arduous task and took a lot of concentration. The humidity of the greenhouse along with the temperature and watering of the plants have to be strictly monitored. At that time, I was into organic gardening using peat moss, dehydrated cow manure and lime. I originally used chemical fertilizers such as 5-10-5 and 10-6-4 but soon realized that the chemical fertilizers were killing the earthworms which were so important for aeration of the soil and their castings for replenishing nutrients as well.

I had joined the Organic Gardening Book Club in Emmaus, Pennsylvania and learned the importance of replenishing nutrients into the soil while gardening at the same time. I even made my own mulch using grass mowing and other greens plus nitrogen fixing bacteria which I bought in a hardware store. I stored the mulch on the hill above my vegetable garden in the back yard. It was really amazing watching the mulch turn a dark color as the plants decayed into a rich loam. I then spread the mulch around the vegetable garden before I did any planting of seeds and plants to be sure the soil was well prepared. I bought wooden stakes for the tomato plants and tied the small plants to the stakes at the bottom and adjusted the ties around the plants as they grew larger.

My tomatoes were simply fabulous! I grew such varieties as Beefsteak and Marglobe tomatoes along with grape tomatoes. The tomatoes were much sweeter and larger than store bought tomatoes. Even the tomato worms liked my tomatoes! (I had to fight them off). At the time, I had an idea of starting an organic hardware store to sell organic items. Although I was only a teenager at the time, I was always looking ahead to the future! Later in life, organic food took off to be a very popular commodity with all grocery stores selling numerous types of vegetables, fruits and a myriad of other categories.

I was also into assembling models of airplanes, rockets and helicopters made out of plastic and balsa wood. I had assembled and painted over 100 models while in high school in the basement of my home. This was a very fascinating hobby and I thoroughly enjoyed it. I especially enjoyed painting all of the plastic models with small bottles of enamel paint which I bought from my local hobby shop. The bottles were sold in sets or by themselves in various sizes and colors. I usually bought sheets of balsa wood and balsa sticks as well and cut them up to assemble the various types of models. I had bought an X-Acto razor knife to cut the balsa wood sheets and sticks and became quite skilled with the knife and enjoyed using it at all times with the hobby.

I also enjoyed classical music. I had purchased numerous LP records of different composers including Beethoven, Hayden, Bach, Chopin, Debussy, and many others. I even assembled a 38watt Heath Kit stereo amplifier and FM tuner which I bought and used a soldering iron to assemble the electronic components.

Since I did not have any speakers for the stereo, I bought several large television cabinets and installed 12" woofer speakers in the cabinets. It worked great! I listened to the classical composers for hours. I especially enjoyed Chopin's piano concertos since they were so relaxing!

I had purchased a guitar and tried to teach myself how to play it. Unfortunately, I was not very good at playing the guitar. My parents had tried to have a piano teacher teach me how to play the piano back in Seattle. However, after two weeks, I asked my parents to stop the instruction since I was not interested.

In high school, I played the clarinet and flute for a little bit but lost interest as well. I even paid for some clarinet and saxophone lessons but stopped as well. I guess that playing musical instruments was not my forte!

One of my high school classmates in the 7th grade was from Kentucky. He simply loved country and western music and played it all of the time. This became the basis for my love for the music in later years. I loved listening to Johnny Cash, Waylon Jennings, Merle Haggard, Dolly Parton, Willie Nelson, and especially Jim Reeves. I have their CD's in my car and play them all of the time. I used to watch the Grand Old Opry which originated from Tennessee on the television and vowed one day to travel to Nashville to see it in person. One day, I will!

One of my friends was interested in astronomy. I joined him on several occasions with his father during the evening to observe the stars at night with his reflective telescope. We observed the big dipper, little dipper and other star formations. It was really fascinating to have a magnified look at the stars in the heavens!

I learned the difference between reflective and refractive telescopes at the time. Little did I know that I would work for NASA (National Aeronautics and Space Administration) years later during the Mercury, Gemini and Apollo programs in the Washington, D.C. Headquarters office of the agency.

In my high school biology class, I was introduced to microscopes. I thoroughly enjoyed using microscopes to observe small plant cells and other items. I had purchased my own Chemcraft microscope to look at vorticella and amoeba microscopic one-celled animals which I had obtained from a nearby pond.

I had purchased a Chemcraft chemistry set as well and used to look at the various chemicals under the microscope. I even used stains to stain the wings of grasshoppers which I had caught to look at the structure of the wings.

I had set up my microscope in the basement of my home since it was very quiet. I had obtained a large sheet of asbestos by calling an asbestos manufacturer which was very generous in shipping the asbestos sheet to me free of charge! The asbestos sheet was ½ inch thick and eight feet square.

I placed the asbestos sheet on top of a large cabinet with shelves. I put the microscope on top of the asbestos sheet since I was using various types of chemicals and acids in my experiments.

It was not known at that time that asbestos was very dangerous and could lead to asbestosis or mesothelioma. I just went about with my experiments, not knowing about the hidden danger of the product. Years later, I threw away the asbestos sheet since it was not safe to keep around the house.

In later years, I had worked at OSHA, the Occupational Safety and Health Administration, in Washington, D.C. As a Safety Specialist, I was responsible for investigating the presence of asbestos in the OSHA Headquarters Office.I supervised the installation of plastic sheeting along with special equipment to monitor the presence of asbestos in the air while maintaining a negative pressure.

I even investigated the garage in the basement of the headquarters building for carbon monoxide levels since the employees on the lower office levels were complaining of headaches. I discovered that the eight foot exhaust fans were installed in a reverse position in the garage which blew exhaust fumes to the office levels above instead of exhausting the fumes outside of the building. Needless to say, I instructed the engineers to reverse the fans and the problem was immediately solved!

I had also discovered cracks in the flooring of the building and met with one of the civil engineers to discuss the problem. He gave me a bag of concrete floor samples which were only several inches thick. The civil engineer stated that the construction company had cheated by using a very thin concrete flooring to save money and make more profit for the company.

I alerted the head of OSHA at that time, 1973, and we had an official investigation to determine the corrective action to be made. We met with officials of the GSA, General Services Administration, but little if anything had resulted from our meeting due to the political nature of the GSA at that time!

During the same meeting, I had informed the GSA officials that rats were eating the telephone cables throughout the offices. The GSA officials did not believe me until I put on rubber gloves and pulled gnawed telephone cables out of a paper bag I had brought with me. This demonstration had the desired effect of making my point but there was no serious follow-up by the GSA! Apparently the agency officials felt they were immune from any valid complaints from other federal agencies! The rats just kept on eating the telephone cables and enjoying their meals.

When I was a teenager, I was also into making firecrackers and rockets out of my own homemade gunpowder. I learned how to make gunpowder with potassium nitrate, sulfur and charcoal which I mixed in the basement of my home.

When I tested the mixture by igniting a small amount, the entire basement was filled with smoke. My parents were not too pleased at the constant amount of smoke in the basement!

I even ran an electrical wire out of the basement window to the back yard and set off an explosive device using a piece of Jetex fuse and an empty wine bottle stopper inside a metal saucepan. What a bang that was!

Unfortunately, a house fuse burned out on occasion due to the electrical surge with the long extension cord which I used to detonate the explosive device. My parents were not pleased! My mother was especially annoyed at the smoke in the basement being absorbed by the laundry hanging on lines to dry.

In my Junior year of high school, I had formed the Wheaton Rocket Society, composed of my friends who were interested in making and firing rockets. We worked with a mixture of zinc powder and sulfur for our solid propellant mixture.

My father arranged for us to fire our rocket during a demonstration at the Army's Camp A.P. Hill in Virginia. We had used the Army's recommended formula for the zinc and sulfur instead of the formula I had developed. Unfortunately, the Army's formula did not work and our rocket never left the ground.

I had studied about rocketry and fabricated the rocket using a standard dellavalle rocket nozzle design which I had made at a local company. I even had the nozzle gold plated! At that time, the price of gold was only about $25.00 per ounce. I don't know what happened to my gold plated nozzle but I am sure someone is enjoying it!

One time, I had the idea of attaching booster rockets to a rocket to give it an additional boost during takeoff. I even fabricated a model which I had made of tubular steel and sheet metal and brought it to school in a brown paper bag to show my science teacher. I was too shy at the time to show my teacher and simply brought it home. In later years, someone had developed booster rockets so I felt vindicated!

Since I was developing my own fuel, I even used potassium chlorate instead of potassium nitrate to give my rockets more power. I also developed a mixture of gunpowder combined with ethanol and gasoline. This was a very flammable mixture and I was very careful to avoid being burned when I ignited my rockets. One of my friends burned his hands by grinding potassium nitrate, sulfur and charcoal all together with his mortar and pestle instead of separately. He didn't understand that friction between gunpowder components can easily ignite them just as with a match or fuse!

I also used potassium perchlorate which was a stronger oxidizer than potassium chlorate. It cost a little more to purchase but I felt that the additional cost was worth it!

I used to buy my chemicals at a company in Silver Spring. I rode my bike to the company since it was only about half an hour ride from my home. I had no problem buying chemicals even though I was 15 or 16 years old at that time. There were no regulations governing the purchase of such chemicals in the 50's. I was even able to order sulfuric acid and had it delivered to my home via Railway Express!

At the same time, I had developed fuel using asphalt oil along with potassium perchlorate. This mixture was known as Galcit and was used in JATO bottles known as "Jet Assist Take Off" for such rockets as the Bomarc Rocket. This rocket fuel was very smoky so I didn't use much of the mixture.

At the time, I was intrigued with asphalt oil and asphalt paving as well. I was even considering attending the University of Maryland at College Park to study civil engineering at their Asphalt Institute. I never moved ahead with this idea since I decided to attend Purdue University in West Lafayette, Indiana instead. One of my Wheaton High School classmates asked me to be his roommate so this is the reason why I applied to Purdue University and was admitted in my senior year of high school in an early admission procedure.

I won my Wheaton High School Science Fair 3rd place award with my project called "Ex Ga Fo Pa", which stood for Exhaust Gas Formation Pattern. I had calculated the range of my rockets by using the base angle of the frustum of the exhaust pattern. One of the judges had told my science teacher that the information which I had developed was "classified" by the U.S. Government.

Apparently, my research was in fact valid and I was amazed at this fact! I probably could have been a rocket scientist! At one time, I contemplated becoming an aeronautical engineer and thought about joining the American Rocket Society while in college. However, I never pushed forward with this thought.

On June 15, 1961, I gave the benediction to my Wheaton High School's graduation. I was at the top of my graduation class and was happy to be selected for this honor:

Let us bow our heads. Dear Lord, please protect us and guide us to a rewarding future through hard work and your Divine guidance. Please watch over us and inspire us to succeed in all of our endeavors. Amen."

The graduation was held outside on the football field on a beautiful, sunny day. All of our families and friends were present. Our school colors of crimson and gold were flowing with our robes being worn by all graduates. When we graduated, the tassel at the top of the hat was moved to the opposite side.

My father had worked for the Air Force Office of Scientific Research (AFOSR) which was located on the mall in Washington, D.C. He was employed as a civilian with the U.S. Government. The buildings were old buildings, constructed during World War II and were originally meant to be temporary quarters only.

I had passed my Civil Service exam in 1961 after completing high school and obtained my first U.S. Government job with the help of my father, in the same organization in which he worked, for my summer employment.

One of the Lieutenant Colonels working in my office created quite a stir when he always wore his U.S. Air Force uniform with sandals instead of the required "low quarters" or dress black shoes. He was obviously "out of uniform" but that didn't seem to bother him. Seeing him in sandals reminds me of one of the characters in the movie Good Morning Vietnam with Robin Williams!

I worked as a GS-2 clerk typist for two summers in my father's organization. I had passed my clerk typist exam at Bolling Air Force Base in Washington, D.C. with a 95% grade. I had typing in high school and was very happy to be able to type all of my college papers later on with my Smith Corona Corsair portable typewriter. I would later on graduate to an electric typewriter in the U.S. Government offices where I worked during my summer employment positions.

I even worked at a graphics company in Silver Spring, Maryland at a part-time job in typesetting. This was a very interesting job which prepared me for my future employment with NASA in graphic arts and illustration from 1963 to 1965 during the summer months.

I had worked as a GS-3 clerk typist as well with NASA but performed such work as producing viewgraphs using an Ozalid machine which used an ammonia compound. I also worked in a photographic dark room where I learned how to develop and print photographs used in the space program.

I was actively working on viewgraphs which were projected from the rear onto three eight foot screens before scientists sitting in a theatre style room during project and program reviews of various space programs such as Mercury, Gemini and Apollo.

I remember seeing plans for the Lunar Lander and its prototype at the Goddard Space Flight Center at Greenbelt, Maryland. The Goddard Space Flight Center was composed of very large buildings designed to construct and display large space vehicles for various space missions. It was named after Dr. Robert H. Goddard, the father of modern rocketry.

I attended Purdue University in West Lafayette Indiana. On graduation day, June 5, 1966, my class graduated inside our auditorium. I had majored in Sociology with a minor in Political Science. I chose this combination purposely since I had the intention of going into politics.

When I was a senior in high school in 1960, I had volunteered to work in Congressman John R. Foley's re-election campaign for U.S. Congress in Maryland's 6th Congressional District. At the same time, I volunteered to work in Senator John F. Kennedy's campaign for president.

I had formed a Young Democrat's Club in Wheaton and recruited friends and supporters of Congressman Foley and Senator Kennedy. Congressman Foley had a cute campaign tactic of stapling teabags to campaign letters alleging, "taxation without representation".

We had delivered the letters door-to-door in Wheaton and urged everyone to vote for Congressman Foley. Unfortunately, he was the only Democratic congressman to lose his seat in 1960

During Senator Kennedy's campaign for president in 1960, I was fortunate to see him up close at Blair High School in Silver Spring, Maryland. I was only 15 feet away amidst a throng of screaming teenage girls behind a roped-off area when he gave a speech. He was so popular and handsome that the teenage girls treated him like a rock star!

I later saw President Kennedy outside on the White House grounds in the summer of 1963 when I was working at NASA Headquarters in Washington, D.C., during a summer job between college semesters. We were asked if anyone wanted to go to the White House to see President Kennedy give a speech.

This was the routine back then when a crowd was desired for a politician's speech. Of course, I volunteered since who didn't want to see the President of the United States?

When I saw President Kennedy, he had aged considerably with gray hair and jowls hanging down his throat. Since the presidency of the United States is one of the most stressful jobs in the world, it's no wonder that President Kennedy showed the effects of the job.

I also saw Vice President Rockefeller give a speech at the Old Executive Office Building in Washington, D.C., also having been asked if I wanted to attend to form an audience. Vice President Rockefeller died of an apparent heart attack in his office at a later date.

I was in college in 1963 on November 22nd when I heard the horrible news that President Kennedy was assassinated. I was in a laundromat when a fellow classmate ran in to say that President Kennedy was shot. I returned to my room and immediately turned on the radio to hear the news: "President Kennedy was dead from a gunshot wound in Texas".

Needless to say, everyone on campus and throughout the United States was devastated. President Kennedy was our president and the leader of the free world who had stood up to the Russians over the Cuban missile crisis and now he was dead. It was especially meaningful to me since I had just seen him in person during the summer of 1963. And now, he was dead!

When President Kennedy was sworn in as president in 1961, I had sent him a letter of congratulations. I received a letter from one of his assistants acknowledging my letter and felt happy to have received this acknowledgement from the President of the United States.\

While studying at Purdue University in 1964, a classmate of mine asked me to volunteer in Roger D. Branigin's campaign to become governor of Indiana. He was a close relative of my classmate and since I had experience as a campaigner in both President Kennedy's and Representative Foley's campaigns, I agreed to participate. Roger Branigin was in fact elected governor of Indiana and served for four years from 1965 to 1969.

I had worked at NASA Headquarters in Washington, D.C. during the summers from 1963 to 1965. The Administrator of NASA at that time was James E. Webb. He was a very strong Administrator. Once, I was present when he tossed out a group of U.S. Representatives from an upstairs briefing room into the adjoining hallway. I believe that he may have been unhappy with their comments about the space program. It was a little shocking to see U.S. Representatives just thrown out of a briefing room. But if you are an administrator of an important federal agency, I guess that you have certain privileges!

I was privileged to see the first walk in space in color which showed the gold colored face shield of the astronaut. The film was very majestic since it showed the astronaut moving around in slow motion with no sound. The color was simply astounding and the space walk was simply surreal!

I met astronaut Walter Schirra at NASA Headquarters and obtained his autograph before he went into a meeting in 1963 and placed it in my NASA scrapbook. Astronaut Schirra met President Kennedy at the White House along with his whole family after his mission on the Mercury Program on October 16, 1962.

In the spring of 1966, the Vietnam War was in full swing. I had two years of Army ROTC, Reserve Officer Training Corps, and didn't go for an additional two years to obtain a 2nd Lieutenant's commission because I saw a senior ROTC cadet berating an Army Sergeant who was working at Purdue University as part of the permanent cadre. I felt that this was highly improper for someone, who wasn't even an officer yet, to treat an Army Sergeant unprofessionally without the proper respect due.

I took and passed my battery of Army exams including math and English and passed with, "flying colors". I also passed my OCS exam and I enlisted in the Army on June 10, 1966, five days after graduating from Purdue as a "College Option" candidate with Basic Combat Training, Advanced Infantry Training, and Infantry Officer Candidate School all scheduled to commence upon successful completion of each segment, all printed on one set of orders.

All of my classmates were college graduates, the last class of this type to be enrolled before "Project 100,000" was due to commence with underprivileged youngsters to be drafted into the Army for service in Vietnam.

I was sworn into the Army along with a group of other enlistees as a Private E-1, the lowest rank in the Army. I was appointed, "train commander", to be in charge of other enlistees on the way from Indiana to Fort Jackson, South Carolina for Basic Combat Training, an eight week period of training.

My group was placed in a reception center for one week prior to basic training to be fitted for our fatigues and to take turns in our barracks as "CQ" or Charge of Quarter for the evening, learning Army procedures. As CQ, we had to take turns staying up all night and making a log of any occurrences during the evening that may impact on the safety of our fellow soldiers.

When we went to the mess hall to eat, we were told, "Take all you want but eat all you take." This made me think before I selected my food since I didn't want to get in trouble by having any food left on my plate. In addition, while in the chow line, we were asked by the enlisted army servers whether we were RA (Regular Army) or NG (National Guard) enlistees. I replied RA, of course, since I had enlisted in the regular army.

The permanent cadre serving us food applauded those of us in the Regular Army. However, those soldiers who were in the National Guard were called, "No Good", instead of National Guard. I felt that this was very disrespectful to the National Guard enlistees. We were all in the Army and I didn't see any reason to disparage any of us just because of our particular category which we entered on active duty.

During the first week of basic training, we had to go on, "Police Call," which was a euphemism for picking up grass, cigarette butts and other trash on the ground with our bare fingers. My fingers were stained green from the grass and it felt like harassment to me. However, you just can't complain if you are a new recruit with a job to do!

The Army corporal in charge was busted from Staff Sergeant E-6 to Corporal E-4. He had a very demeaning attitude towards the recruits. When it came time for issuance of our military I.D.'s, he stood behind a stand outside and called each recruit's name. When someone answered, the corporal tossed the I.D. on the ground as if he were throwing a Frisbee and each recruit had to run and pick up his I.D.

I felt that this was no way to issue I.D.'s to new recruits and it reflected unfavorably upon the U.S. Army. However, we had no basis to comment since we were all new to the U.S. Army and didn't want to make a scene!

I was given temporary Sergeant E-5 stripes on my sleeve since I was a college graduate with very high test scores on the Army entrance exam. However, as soon as I failed my PCPT (Physical Combat Proficiency Test), I immediately lost my stripes. I was then placed in the, "Goon Platoon", with others who failed the PCPT Test as well. Of course, it was very embarrassing to not only fail the PCPT test but to be placed in a group of failures!

My platoon sergeant was constantly berating me as I was in the, "front leaning rest position," otherwise known as the push-up position. He shouted at me, "You can't even do push-ups, you are so fat and weak. How are you ever going to make it in this man's Army? You can't even pass the PCPT Test, you are so slow! You ran the mile in 10 ½ minutes. I can walk faster than you can run!" I replied, "Yes sir!"

My platoon sergeant replied, "Don't call me sir! I work for a living!" I replied, "Yes Sergeant" and he was satisfied. After being berated by my platoon sergeant, I vowed to do much better to improve myself. Again, I was very embarrassed by my platoon sergeant but knew that he was only doing his job!

I entered the Army weighing 183 pounds and went down to 167 pounds in only six weeks. I ran the mile in 6 ½ minutes and was the best in my platoon at the hand grenade or "remagen" range with the highest score of anyone. My platoon sergeant was simply amazed at my mile run and I felt exonerated!

We did a lot of running in basic training. Our platoon sergeants normally ran with us as we sang, "I want to be an Airborne Ranger, I want to live a life of danger; Airborne Ranger, life of danger".

I gained a lot of respect for Army Drill Sergeants. They had to take care of all of the recruits in all respects. As a matter of fact, when I began basic training, our platoon sergeant told us, "I am your father and mother". With this statement, we all felt overwhelmed at the prospect of our parents being replaced by our platoon sergeant! However, we knew that they had a lot of responsibility in grooming future officers since we were all bound for OCS, Officer Candidate School, upon completion of basic training.

I remember one touching event when I was with two drill sergeants when they asked me if I was going to treat sergeants with respect when I become an officer. I replied, "Of course I am. We are all working together as a team". They were very happy to hear this.

I learned later on that sergeants are the backbone of the Army and deserve respect at all times. Too often, however, this is not the case. Of course, there must always be respect between officers and non-commissioned officers (NCO'S) at all times if the Army is going to be run well. As a matter of fact, while serving in Eighth U.S. Army in South Korea, I learned that senior officers and senior NCO's are often good friends!

Our Company Commander in basic training was an excellent commander. One thing, however, stuck out in my memory; he was a captain who rode his motorcycle alongside us when we ran our two mile run every morning instead of running with us as did our drill sergeants. This struck me as somewhat odd, that our Company Commander was too lazy to run with us. I felt that this was highly improper but was unable to do anything about it since it was not my place. It was so strange!

During our many trips in a five ton Army truck, we all sat on wooden benches in rows. We were always transported in five ton Army trucks during field exercises. We liked to perform skits during the ride and I had one which I developed.

One of my buddies and I performed the skit when he pretended to select me for a "detail", the Army term for a work assignment. My buddy said to me, "I have some bad news for you!" I replied, "What is it?" He said, "I have a detail for you!" Reacting with pretended shock, I answered, "Oh God no", opening my mouth and eyes with feigned horror. All of my buddies on the truck always broke out in loud laughter. We repeated this drama numerous times during our training exercises and always had good results!

As a matter of fact, during one of our field exercises we asked our platoon sergeant if we could perform a skit. The sergeant said okay in order to break up the serious mood of the exercise. We then performed the skit with a song called, "Brassiere!", which was sung to the tune of "Marie". Here is the song:

> "Brassiere, you hold those things we love so dear,
>
> And when they brush against my ears,
>
> My pecker goes into high gear, brassiere

The song is repeated several times for effect. As a matter of fact, one of my buddies had secretly hidden a real brassiere in his back pack and put it on during the song. We all opened up our arms and kneeled down during the performance to emphasize our feelings about the subject.

After we finished the song, our entire company burst into laughter with our platoon sergeants especially enjoying the performance. It was really a lot of fun doing the skit and we really felt the camaraderie of being together in the Army.

When our platoon sergeant came looking for us for details, we all split; not wanting to go on details. One of our fellow recruits had the best possible hiding place; in bed! He would lie down in bed with the blanket and sheet on top of him and lie perfectly still. When he was lying down, you couldn't see his body, he lay so perfectly flat. It was simply amazing and a perfect place to hide.

The same person would perch himself on top of the shelves about seven feet above the floor and pretend to be a gargoyle. We didn't think that he had his wits about him! However, we weren't in any position to comment on our fellow recruits.

Upon completion of Basic Combat Training (BCT) for eight weeks, I had to go to AIT which I thought meant Advanced Individual Training. However, I soon learned that for me, AIT meant Advanced Infantry Training, a prelude to Infantry OCS which I was slated to attend for 25 weeks. However, I really enjoyed AIT since I qualified as an Expert Marksman with my favorite M-60 machine gun and M-14 rifle.

I was the best in my company with the M-60 and even carried it on field exercises during the winter months. I remember holding the M-60 while asleep on the frozen ground outside with only a rubber poncho to keep me warm at night. The rubber poncho really did work to keep yourself warm with your body supplying all of the heat necessary.

I laid down in a depression in the ground under a tree for shelter and was very comfortable during the evening. My platoon sergeant recommended that I find a depression in the ground since it would be more comfortable. He was right!

While enrolled in OCS, we had to spit shine our floors in our rooms in addition to spit shining our boots and shoes. Our Tactical Officers (we called them TAC Officers) used to come into our rooms after we spit shined the floors and grind their boots into the floors for harassment purposes. Needless to say, we were not happy campers at the time. However, who were we to complain.

One of my classmates had the last name of Roach. This simply threw the senior candidates into a frenzy! The senior candidates took great joy at harassing us by having us lie upside down on our bunk beds with our arms and legs in the air in the position of a dying cockroach. With our classmate having Roach for his last name, this simply made their harassment more enjoyable; except for our classmate, of course!

Infantry OCS was divided into three segments during the 25 week period. In the first segment, we were basic candidates. In the second segment, we were intermediate candidates. And in the third segment, we were senior candidates.

Normally, the senior candidates could harass other lower level candidates but during our period of OCS, harassment was discontinued when we became senior candidates. Both the basic and intermediate candidates wore black helmet liners but the senior candidates wore blue helmet liners. If you are a lower level candidate, seeing a blue helmet liner was scary indeed since you felt intimidated!

The Tactical Officers were all commissioned officers, second lieutenants, who had gone through OCS as well and knew all of the tricks. Speaking of tricks, several candidates were very adept at sneaking pizza into our barracks using trash cans. I don't know how they did this but they got away with it.

Speaking of pizza, during basic training we were not authorized to go to the snack bar before the sixth week. However, I managed go to the snack bar with one of my classmates to have pizza in the third week. We never got caught but felt somewhat guilty at the time. However, if you have a craving for pizza, like in OCS, you sometimes take chances!

About halfway during our training, we were awakened by the TAC officers during the middle of the night with a lot of shouting, "Get out of the sack and put on your gear".

We were brought to the famous Raider's Creek outside our barracks for a "low crawl" with full combat gear. The creek was a sewer outlet and you can imagine our feelings with our faces down in the creek with our heavy gear on at the same time.

However, this was part of the OCS regimen; tough training to build officers Some of us, however, failed to comprehend how "low crawling" through a sewer outlet was training to build officers. However, we were in no position to question our superior officers.

In Infantry OCS, we were all taught the slogan, "Follow me; I am infantry!" We were taught to be leaders of men and this philosophy stuck with me during the entire period of our training.

At the end of the 25 week period, we were called into the Company Commander's office who was a first lieutenant. He asked me, "Do you know why I called you into my office?" I replied, "Sir, no sir". He said, "I called you into my office because I don't think that you would make a good officer. I think that you would like an opportunity to resign from OCS and return to being enlisted. Isn't this what you would like to do, Candidate? Why don't you resign, Candidate?"

I replied, "Sir, no sir". The Company Commander said, "I have been observing you, Candidate, and I don't think that you have what it takes to lead men. Do you think that you could lead men in combat, Candidate?" I replied, "Sir, yes sir". The Company Commander replied, "Well, we'll see, Candidate. I'll have to think about this. You're dismissed".

Other Candidates were grilled in this manner by our Company Commander and did not succumb to this ruse except one of my classmates and close friend. I later met him and received a very cordial military salute from him when I became a second lieutenant and he was a Specialist E-5, retaining our OCS enlisted rank. I felt somewhat sad that he had left OCS since he had the highest academic ranking of anyone in our company and would have made an outstanding officer.

I graduated from Infantry OCS on April 24, 1967, along with my buddies, many of whom completed basic training and advanced infantry training with me at Ft. Jackson. We all placed a second lieutenant insignia gold bar inside our hats in the event of our graduation. Once graduating, we would remove the gold bar and pin it outside of our hat.

We were all nervous and worried about whether we would in fact graduate. We were all senior candidates and our families were present and the event was complemented with marching bands and all of the officers present including the commanding general.

The brigade commander began speaking to the battalion commander, 94th Officer Candidate Battalion, "Have the members of your battalion completed all of the requirements to become commissioned as second lieutenants?" The battalion commander replied, "Sir, I am proud to say that all of the senior candidates of the 94th Officer Candidates Battalion have completed all of their requirements and I recommend that all of the senior candidates be commissioned as second lieutenants.

The brigade commander then spoke to the commanding general, "Sir, I recommend that all of the senior candidates of the 94th Officer Candidate Battalion be duly commissioned as second lieutenants in the U.S. Army". The commanding general then replied, "I accept your recommendation and hereby confer the rank of second lieutenant to all members of the 94th Officer Candidate Battalion with the authority of the President of the United States".

With that announcement, all members of my battalion threw our hats into the air and, upon catching them, took out the second lieutenant gold bar and pinned it to the outside of our hat, thus ending 25 grueling weeks of training.

Our barracks at Ft. Benning was located adjacent to the jump towers used for airborne training. The period of airborne training was for only three weeks and I honestly considered going airborne. However, when I saw individuals with broken legs and hanging halfway down the jump tower, dangling from a line, I changed my mind.

I even considered applying for the Green Berets but instead, applied for a branch transfer to the Adjutants General Corps since I felt that this was more suited to my liking with personnel and administration at the core of this branch of the Army. We referred to the Adjutants General Corps shield as the "shield of splendor" and enjoyed wearing the shield on our uniform at all times!

After completing Infantry OCS and transferring to the Adjutants General Corps, known as AGC, I attended a five week AGC school at Ft. Benjamin Harrison, Indiana. I was happy to return to Indiana since I graduated from Purdue University at West Lafayette, Indiana. I learned the principles of effective writing at the school along with other administrative duties and was happy with my branch transfer.

I had requested an assignment near my home for my first Army assignment. My request was fulfilled with an assignment at Aberdeen Proving Ground in Aberdeen, Maryland. I was assigned to the U.S. Army Ordinance Center and School as an AGC officer.

Aside from working on personnel and administrative duties, I was assigned the responsibility of investigating cases where individuals had written letters to the President, Senators or Congressmen complaining about their treatment in the Army or other matters. I investigated each case by talking with the serviceman and obtaining all of the information I could with recommendations for solution. I then had to staff the reply for the Commanding General through six officers above me. This took some time since each officer changed my reply to his own liking.

I recommended to my supervisor that the amount of officers which needed to review my letter be reduced to two officers only and this was approved. This was the most interesting and fulfilling of my assignment at Aberdeen Proving Ground. I was also assigned the duty of Postal Officer. I used to visit the military post office and conduct inspections of the postal employees and their procedures to ensure that they were following regulations.

After a one-year assignment at Aberdeen Proving Ground, we had a new supervisor who was a major, the same rank as our previous supervisor. There were five second lieutenants in my group who reported to the major. When he came on board, the major said, "Gentlemen, you need to make me look good on my OER, Officer's Evaluation Report, since this is my primary concern".

After the staff meeting when we heard our supervisor's pronouncement, we all met separately to discuss what he had said. I first spoke to the group and said, "I don't understand why the major only cares about himself. Why doesn't he care about us?" Another member of our group said, "I agree with you. All I can say is that I am going to volunteer for Vietnam. The major has no business just taking care of himself and ignoring our needs!" The rest of our staff agreed. We all agreed to volunteer for Vietnam at the same time so the major will be left without a staff.

Within a month, all members of our staff had been assigned overseas, leaving the major without a staff. I volunteered for Vietnam as well but was told that I would have to extend my service obligation for an additional year in the Army in order to be assigned to Vietnam.

I had my choice of Vietnam, Korea or Thailand at the time for an overseas assignment. I didn't feel like extending my service period for an additional year, especially for an assignment in Vietnam where the life expectancy of second lieutenants at the time was only five minutes. As a matter of fact, one of my OCS classmates was killed by a sniper as he was walking down the stairs of his airplane upon arrival in Vietnam. I felt especially sad when this happened.

If I were assigned to Europe, I would have extended my service obligation for an additional year. But Vietnam; no way! Instead, I called the Office of Personnel Operations, known as OPO, and asked to be assigned to Korea. Within nine days from my phone call, I was assigned to Korea!

My parents had seen me off at Dulles International Airport in Virginia. I remember the solemn occasion with my mother dabbing her eyes and embracing both of my parents in my Army uniform. I felt a little guilty at leaving them but wanted to serve our country the best that I could.

I arrived in South Korea in April 1968, arriving on a military transport plane at Kimpo Air Base in Seoul. While on the plane ride, I was studying the Korean language using an Army pamphlet. We were given a box lunch to eat on board the long flight consisting of sandwiches and a drink. My ears were congested due to a cold when I left the U.S. which contributed to a partial loss of hearing for several weeks after my arrival. Hence forward, I would require a decongestant on all future flights to keep my ears clear.

Upon arrival at the air base, I was escorted with all other military personnel to a medical station. At the medical station, I was told that I was to receive not one but two shots of gamma globulin medication, one in each butt. I was told that the shots were part of an experimental procedure to ward off the effects of malaria.

Each shot was huge with almost one ounce or more of serum. They were painful also and I was incredulous at this happening just as I arrived in Korea, fatigued from the long trip and combined with jet lag. However I had no choice since I had to follow orders from a medical doctor who outranked me.

I was immediately transported by Army bus to the 38th Replacement Battalion at Bupyong. Since it was very cold in Korea with frozen dirt roads, the ride was very bumpy. I was seated at the back of the bus with two very sore butts on a bumpy, frozen road! It was a very painful trip to Bupyong, lasting several hours! I couldn't wait to get off the bus and change from my Class A uniform.

I was assigned to Headquarters, I Corps Group in Uijongbu, near the DMZ, as an Assistant Adjutant General in the command. My immediate supervisor was a Lieutenant Colonel and his supervisor was a Colonel. They were both seated in front of our Quonset hut which was a temporary building set up during the Korean war. The Quonset huts needed to be heated by space heaters during the winter but were generally comfortable.

I was placed in charge of another second lieutenant since I was commissioned in the morning and he was commissioned in the afternoon. In other words, I had "date of rank" over the other officer by virtue of having been commissioned several hours before him. This concept of Army life was new to me and very interesting.

As a newly arrived officer in the command, I was to be introduced during the monthly, "Hail and Farewell Ceremony," a standard occurrence at all Army bases worldwide. The monthly ceremony normally takes several hours to complete with everyone drinking liquor and mingling together.

I was not enthusiastic about these ceremonies and expressed my displeasure to other officers. I especially didn't like to stand up while drinking alcoholic beverages since it is very difficult to speak intelligently and coherently when drinking, let alone keeping your balance.

Having lost patience in the drinking and mingling, I left the group. Soon afterwards, my name was called, "We would like to welcome LT

Seiden into the command. LT Seiden? Where are you? Are you here?" There was no response, of course, since I left the group due to boredom.

The following morning, I was called into my two immediate superior officer's office. I suddenly realized that my action the day before was a mistake. The Lieutenant Colonel had a smirk on his face since he was amused at my leaving the Hail and Farewell Ceremony before my name was called as a new arrival in the command. However, the Colonel was more serious and was not amused at all.

The Colonel asked me, "LT Seiden, why did you leave the Hail and Farewell Ceremony before you were to be introduced to the command?" I replied, "Well, sir, I just felt somewhat bored and didn't feel that it was necessary". The Colonel replied, "LT Seiden, the Hail and Farewell Ceremony is a very important part of Army life and you should appreciate this during your Army career. Don't let this happen again!"

I replied, "Yes sir! I won't let it happen again!" After meeting with my superior officers, I realized that I made a mistake and was careful to attend all Hail and Farewell Ceremonies in the future.

When I first arrived in Korea I was really surprised at the lack of developed land in Seoul, the capitol. Driving from Seoul to areas north of the capitol, there was an abundance of barren hills and trees.

I drove an Army jeep from different Eighth U.S. Army compounds around Seoul on several occasions and had to navigate on a number of unpaved roads. All of this would change remarkably in later years!

A job came up for an executive officer position in the 59th Aviation Company a short distance away from where I was working at Hq I Corps (Group) in Uijongbu. I volunteered for the position since I have never had a command position in the Army and since I was trained in Infantry OCS, I felt that I could handle the position.

There were about 100 men in the company composed of Warrant Officers who were aviators and an assemblage of flight mechanics and other support positions. My commanding officer (CO) was a major and I was a first lieutenant. We used to fly around Korea just above the rice paddies, waving to the rice paddy workers below.

Our company had fixed wing Otter aircraft, Huey helicopter gunships and OH47 Observation Helicopters which seated only two occupants. My CO and I used to fly around in the OH47 Observation Helicopters which resembled a large bubble on a stick. My CO was an excellent aviator and I had a lot of confidence in his aviation skills. He was a West Point Military Academy graduate and his father was also, having reached the rank of Major General.

On one occasion, I had a quarrel with a warrant officer and my commanding officer called the warrant officer and myself into his office and placed us at attention and chewed us out for unprofessional behavior.

I realized that we were both at fault for unprofessional behavior and vowed not to repeat this in the future. The warrant officer was a returnee from Vietnam and his wife was recently injured in a terrible car accident by having been thrown through the car windshield. Therefore, he was under a lot of stress and I should have been more understanding at the time.

Since our aviation company was situated close to the DMZ in a designated combat zone, the aviators were required to perform what is called, "auto rotation", once per week. In this maneuver, the aviator flies the Huey Gunship up to about 12,000 feet and turns off the power. As the helicopter descends, the upward draft of the helicopter blades allow for a controlled descent. Just prior to crashing on the ground (I use this term guardedly), the aviator turns on the power and the helicopter blades begin their powered rotation again, allowing the aviator to regain use of the aircraft.

I went on one of these auto rotations only once. As soon as the aviator turned off the power and the helicopter began to plummet, my stomach remained at 12,000 feet, while the helicopter fell like a rock. I vowed never again to go on the auto rotation. It was so scary and my stomach did not appreciate the training!

Having served for one year on active duty in Korea, I decided to become discharged in country and change to a civilian job with the

U.S. Government. In order to do this, I was required by the Army to obtain a Korean tourist visa.

However, the Korean Ministry of Foreign Affairs required military personnel to first become discharged from the Army before being issued a tourist visa, a "Catch 22". This did not perturb me since I was taught to accomplish the mission in the Army at all possible costs.

I, therefore, went to the official at the Korean Ministry of Foreign Affairs who was responsible for issuance of tourist visas on three separate visits. The first two times he denied my request even though I sat directly in front of him, staring at him for one hour each time. On the third visit, the official recognized me when I sat in front of his desk again. He relented and issued me my tourist visa. I guess that he became tired of my staring at him. But I was happy to have accomplished my mission.

I soon was discharged in country and learned that I was only the third officer to accomplish this feat. A four star Army general and a Colonel in the Air Force were discharged in country as well before me.

The Army was very concerned about the four star general being discharged in the command due to his high level security clearance and knowledge of secrets. The worry was that if he were captured by North Korean agents, his knowledge of secrets would be compromised. Fortunately, the general soon returned to the U.S. and this potential threat never materialized.

While working as a civilian employee with the Hq., 2nd Infantry Division, in Munsan, Korea, I decided to apply for a position with the FBI, writing a letter on August 20, 1970, to the FBI.

I received a reply from the Director of the FBI, John Edgar Hoover, dated August 31, 1970, with an application and instructions to apply at my local FBI field office upon my return to the U.S. for a Special Agent position. I never applied to the FBI when I returned to the U.S. but did keep his letter and had it framed for a keepsake. I learned that Director J. Edgar Hoover was not only the longest serving Director of the FBI, but he acted as the agency's Personnel Director, hiring Special Agents himself along with handling other personnel functions.

I was married in Korea after being discharged from the Army. My first child, Elizabeth, was born in Korea. My wife and I adopted her brother and niece with the intention of bringing them to the U.S. after completion of my government service.

I brought my brother-in-law to Hawaii in 1972 to have him naturalized as a U.S. Citizen expeditiously before returning to Korea. This was a special procedure available to U.S. Government employees and contractors stationed overseas. My brother-in-law became a U.S. Citizen in only one week and I obtained a U.S. passport for him during that period as well.

I had applied for my niece for a visa at the American Embassy in Seoul. However, the Vice Consul informed me that, since she was not an immediate relative, she was ineligible to receive an immigrant visa. She could only apply for a non-preference category for visa issuance which takes many years to process. Needless to say, we were all very unhappy to leave her in Korea since she was part of our family. I had adopted her and felt that she deserved an immigrant visa.

Since we were scheduled to depart Korea in the spring of 1973, I decided to write a letter to President Nixon to ask for help in the issuance of my niece's visa. Several weeks after writing my letter to President Nixon, I received a phone call from the same Vice Consul who had denied the visa application for my niece. He had called me on a Friday and told me that he had found a visa for her and she would be issued an immigrant visa on Monday. Needless to say, we were overjoyed at this information.

The following Monday morning we met with the Vice Consul. I noticed a cable from the State Department on his desk. I tried to read it upside down and was able to make out the following statement, "The Secretary has directed that an immigrant visa be made available for the following individual".

I thanked the Vice Consul for preparing the visa for my niece and that she will be able to return to the U.S. as a permanent resident along with the rest of my family. I was especially thankful to President Nixon for intervening on behalf of my niece to enable her to accompany us.

I had spent five years in Korea as an Army officer and with the U.S. Government in various administrative positions. I maintained my officer status in the Army Reserve as well and entered on active duty from time-to-time when required by statute to fulfill my military obligation.

After completion of five years of service in Korea I returned to the U.S. in 1973 and found a position with the U.S. Department of Labor after several months in the Occupational Safety and Health Administration, OSHA, in Washington, D.C. The agency was established in 1970 and since I was working as a safety specialist in Eighth U.S. Army, for four years, I felt that this was a logical step to take for my professional development.

I was promoted to Captain after my arrival in the U.S. and served on active duty with several Army installations, including the Pentagon, for a number of years. My mandatory retirement date was 1995 but I later resigned my commission. Had I stayed in the active reserves until 1995, this would have coincided with my U.S. Federal Government retirement date of 1995 from my civilian employment.

Had I stayed in the active reserves, however, I would have been called up to active duty during Desert Storm since my reserve unit was a civil affairs unit with the area objective of the Middle East. No one knew at that time in the early 1970's that the U.S. would become involved militarily in the Middle East. Luckily, I had made a good decision since my family was the most important thing in my life!

After arrival in the U.S. my second child, Susan, was born. She was a welcome addition to our family. We were now a family of six, including my brother-in-law and niece. However, after several years we returned to a family of four when my brother-in-law and niece went to California to join their Korean relatives. They both would later marry and have children of their own.

In 1976, former Congressman Gilbert Gude decided to retire. Having always harbored a desire to go into politics myself, I decided to resign from the U.S. Government and run for U.S. Congress in Maryland's 8th Congressional District which includes the majority of Montgomery County.

In 1975 I ran for the position of Honorary Mayor of Wheaton on a platform of incorporating the town of Silver Spring, Maryland. However, no one wanted to pay more taxes so the incorporation issue was dead on arrival.

I won the election for Honorary Mayor but did not have any official duties. Several Maryland State Senators and Delegates participated in the election along with a number of residents in Wheaton.

We held the election in the Wheaton Triangle area and I placed my campaign poster around the area. It was a beautiful, sunny day and several hundred people showed up for the event.

To kick off my campaign for the U.S. Congress, a fund raiser was organized at the Veterans of Foreign Wars Lodge in Wheaton, Maryland in March 1976. I was a member of the VFW and gave a speech before the assembled audience. The official of the VFW even had me join in singing during the event and I was happy to join in the festivities.

The issues of asbestos and gun control were in vogue at the time and were incorporated into my campaign. I gave several interviews which were broadcast live on the radio and I appeared on live television with the League of Women Voters sponsoring debates among all of the candidates for the congressional seat. My picture was also in The Washington Post during the campaign. I even had campaign buttons and bumper stickers made for my run for Congress.

One of my associates at the U.S. Department of Labor coined my campaign slogan, "I'm Sidin' with Seiden for Congress", which I used on my campaign buttons and bumper stickers. I thought it was a clever slogan and appreciated my associate's ingenuity.

During one of my speeches in Rockville, Maryland, Governor Jerry Brown walked in with a slew of TV cameras and photographers in front of him with bright lights glaring. He asked me if he could give his speech before I finished mine and I quickly agreed and gave up the podium.

Governor Brown was running for president at the time and I wanted to show respect for him. After he gave his speech, I finished my speech.

Governor Brown of California was very popular at the time and continues to be very popular to this date!

About the same time period, President Jimmy Carter was scheduled for a speech as well. Since I was running for the U.S. Congress, I didn't have any qualms about stopping him before his speech to introduce myself and chat about politics. He was very gracious and spoke with me for a few minutes with TV cameras rolling as well. President Carter was running for president in 1976 and won the election. I felt very privileged to have spoken with a future U.S. President in Rockville, Maryland.

I also met Maryland Governor Marvin Mandel during my campaign. I met him at a fund raiser along with his wife. He spoke only several words to me since he was in a hurry but was very polite. His wife was much taller and was very sweet.

Prior to running my campaign for U.S. Congress, I met with Senator Henry M. "Scoop" Jackson at his office in the U.S. Senate. My father had worked with Senator Jackson before he became a U.S. Senator at the Seattle Post Intelligencer Newspaper.

After he became a U.S. Senator, "Scoop" Jackson called my father from time-to-time to chat. I was able to meet Senator Jackson through my father's association with him and rode the train under the U.S. Capitol while he was on his way to cast his vote on some legislation. Senator Jackson told me that he would support me if I won the Democratic primary.

Frank Mankiewicz was also a candidate for congress in my campaign. He was a press aide to Robert Kennedy and National Public Radio President as well. Mr. Mankiewicz was a journalist and lawyer and very highly respected in his profession. We shared a podium for one of our speeches and I was privileged to have met him.

Unfortunately, I was not able to win the primary in April 1976. There were 25 candidates for the 8th Congressional District seat which Congressman Gude vacated. This was the largest number of Candidates to run for an elected position in the history of Maryland's 8th Congressional District and perhaps in all of the United States.

I also met former Senator Paul Sarbanes at his office in the U.S. Senate. He gave me some words of wisdom for my campaign and he told me that he would support me if I won the Democratic nomination for my congressional campaign as well. I enjoyed meeting Senator Sarbanes, having voted for him previously, and supporting his positions as well.

I received a letter dated May 28, 1976, from then Mayor William Donald Schaefer of the City of Baltimore, Maryland. He said in his letter, "I am writing to you to express my sentiments for your unsuccessful bid for a Congressional seat in the Democratic Party. Your campaign attempt was an admirable one, and one in which you should take great pride. Best wishes for the future". I wrote back thanking him for such a wonderful letter. Mayor Schaefer would later become Governor Schaefer of Maryland. I placed his letter in a frame for memory sake!

I also met Katherine Graham, Chairman of the Board of The Washington Post newspaper in 1976 on my campaign trail. She was very gracious and we chatted for a few minutes about my campaign.

Newton Steers, a Republican, won the 1976 congressional race in Montgomery County's Eighth Congressional District. Even though I ran for Congress as a Democrat, we both shared the same political philosophy. I even gave several speeches for Newton as his proxy during the campaign. Newton won the election in 1976 and served only one term as our congressman.

 I began my own consulting business in Wheaton in 1976 after losing my bid for the U.S. Congress. I had a small office space in a private building in downtown Wheaton. I worked alone with my desk, typewriter, file cabinet and sofa as my office equipment.

One day, I was seated behind my desk with my card file in front of me. I was trying to find a phone number of an individual in my card file but didn't know where to look. Suddenly, a card popped up by itself with the exact name and phone number of the individual I was looking for. I was astonished!

I felt that God or an angel had found the name card for me and brought up the card. I felt that God and His angels can read your mind at any time and can provide immediate assistance when needed. I know now that my guardian angel had brought up the card for me. She is always taking care of me at all times!

I decided to move into a larger office in the same building in Wheaton. I had hired two secretaries and five consultants to assist me with my international business. One of my associates with my former agency, the U.S. Department of Labor, was an experienced acupuncturist. Since my office was very large, I agreed to utilize a portion of the office to have her treat patients with acupuncture with such problems as arthritis, bursitis, tendonitis, and many other types of illnesses.

In order to treat patients with acupuncture, we had to purchase several treatment tables and pooled our money together to buy them. Each table cost over $1,000 but they were worth the money!

Even though acupuncturists were not required to be licensed at the time, I felt that it would be a good idea to have a medical doctor oversee our clinic. Luckily, a medical doctor was working in the building and agreed to oversee our clinic. We had numerous patients over the two year period our clinic was in operation. I even had acupuncture administered to myself and was amazed at its effectiveness!

Acupuncture has been in use throughout China for over 5,000 years. It is often combined with acupressure and moxibustion. Acupressue consists of applying pressure to various points throughout the body to relieve pain. Moxibustion consists of burning certain types of herbs in a metal crucible above a point on the body to relieve pain as well.

Designated points on the body to relieve pain are called meridians and can be seen on special medical charts which are normally placed in acupuncture offices. There are perhaps several hundred meridians throughout the body that correspond to specific ailments.

During one of my trips to Taiwan, I was fortunate enough to visit an acupuncturist's office. Since the acupuncturist in my own clinic was from Taiwan and her father practiced acupuncture in Taiwan for 50 years, I thought it suitable to visit such an office to get firsthand experience in witnessing such a procedure.

I followed the acupuncturist, a medical doctor, when he went from room to room holding a handful of acupuncture needles. He skillfully inserted the needles like throwing darts to the designated meridians on each patient who was lying on treatment tables. It was really fascinating at the speed and accuracy with which the doctor inserted the needles. To this date, I have never witnessed such an activity!

During the same trip to Taiwan, I was invited to watch a movie of a woman being operated on to remove a large cyst from one of her breasts. The only anesthesia which she received was from acupuncture needles which were skillfully implanted. She was awake during the entire operation and was sipping a soft drink as well. This was really fantastic!

My acupuncturist had asked me to obtain a medical device from China during my trip which consisted of a battery pack with wires to attach to acupuncture needles to increase the voltage during treatment. I was able to obtain the device in Singapore. Normally, an acupuncturist twists the needles after insertion to a meridian to increase the voltage for effectiveness. The battery pack eliminates this requirement by providing a boost in the voltage automatically.

I received treatments of acupuncture myself from my acupuncturist in our clinic for pain She was excellent in that the pain subsided after a half a dozen treatments. I received acupuncture treatments as well from an American doctor but he could not compare to my own clinic's acupuncturist since she was Taiwanese and was much more experienced in the art.

When having acupuncture, you immediately feel the electric shock type of effect which travels throughout the body. It is really fantastic that needles inserted into a meridian can accomplish so much in so little time without the need for medicine.

This is the immediate benefit of acupuncture, the unnecessary reliance upon medicine for our normal ailments in our body.

I purchased a house in Silver Spring in 1977. It was an old, well-constructed home, having been built for one of President Franklin D. Roosevelt's so called, "Kitchen Cabinet" officials in the early 1930's, I was told by the previous owner. The home was made of brick and stone with a slate roof and copper down spouts. The house had five bedrooms, a detached three-car garage and was situated on one and one third acres. It was a beautiful house with a fireplace, an old-fashioned circular staircase with high plaster walls and was quite spacious.

For the first two years, nothing was amiss. At the beginning of the third year, however, unexplained things began to occur. During one day when I was alone and my family was out of the house, I was watching television in the living room, adjacent to the circular staircase.

I felt that someone was looking at me out of the corner of my left eye. It was an uncomfortable feeling. I immediately turned to my left and saw a ghost on the fourth or fifth step of the stairs watching me. There was someone in the interior of the ghost in color while the exterior of the ghost was in the form of a gray apparition.

I stared at the ghost while it remained on the stairs for four to five seconds. Suddenly, the ghost speeded up the stairs like a comet and disappeared. I was really scared since this was my first sighting of a real ghost. I really couldn't tell whether the ghost was a male or female but estimated that it was about four to four and one-half feet tall. I suspect that the ghost was a child due to its small size.

The very next day the same ghost appeared when I was alone watching television. Again, when I looked at the ghost, it zipped up the stairs with no apparent noise. I didn't try to talk to the ghost since I was so scared.

On another occasion, I was again watching television alone. Suddenly, someone tapped me on my left shoulder. Needless to say, I was alarmed and scared at the same time. Again, I was powerless to do anything, the same feeling as the visitation by the ghost.

The same event occurred the very next day as with the visitation of the ghost. This time, prior to being tapped on my left shoulder, I felt a chill in the air. I didn't feel a need to say anything out loud since I thought that it wouldn't make any difference.

I was slowly getting used to paranormal experiences with visitations by two ghosts and two taps on my shoulder, all on my left side. In retrospect, I felt later that my guardian angel had tapped me on my left shoulder to show that she was always with me. My guardian angel, I call her "Divine", has touched me on many occasions all around the world!

On yet another occasion, I was home alone watching television when I heard someone walking upstairs. I was startled at this occurrence and wondered who it may be. This happened several more times and my family heard the walking as well but were powerless to do anything about it.

The ghosts that appeared in my house were not poltergeists since they did not harm my family. They were obviously friendly ghosts and may have simply been curious. However, we were all scared when they did appear or start walking on the floor above.

On another occasion, my son David, who was 1 ½ at the time, had complained that his bed was shaking during the middle of the night. I told David to go back to sleep, not realizing that a spiritual entity had probably shaken his bed.

As a matter of fact, his room was painted black before I purchased the house. I had his room repainted with three coats of white paint to cover the black walls. Before I purchased the house, I learned that the previous owner's children were involved in the occult or witchcraft. I really didn't believe this piece of information but came to realize that it might have been true!

On still another occasion Susan saw a ghost go through the walls while calling her name. Susan was the only member of my family to have heard her name called, let alone a voice heard from a spiritual entity. I don't know why Susan was singled out for this type of spiritual encounter. She was scared out of her wits, of course, as we all were with such paranormal experiences.

One night, I was alone in my bedroom when the door handle began to turn. The doors in the house were fitted with old-fashioned crank-style doorknobs. Susan was in her bedroom about 30 feet down the hall. I thought that Susan was playing a prank on me and opened my door to see if she was on the other side. At the same time, Susan opened her door and asked me if I turned her door handle. When we both realized that neither of us had turned each other's door handle, a sudden chill overcame both of us. Either a ghost with two very long arms turned our door handles simultaneously or two ghosts were involved in scaring us!

It was indeed very unnerving to be living with ghosts. You never know when they would appear. I suspect that two ghosts were turning our door handles at the same time, having fun at our expense. I also suspected that both ghosts were children having fun!

I pray every night to God to bless my family and to protect them. During one evening, I was praying to God to see his face. I prayed very hard for several hours and was very happy to actually see God's face. God showed me both sides of his face, first the left side and then the right side. He had a large gray beard and gray mustache and his face was gray in color as well. His eyes were piercing and I had a sudden feeling that God was saying to me, "Who are you to look upon the face of God?"

I knew then that it was wrong of me to ask to see God's face since we must always believe in God and love God as we love our fellow men and women. God's face appeared to me for only five to ten seconds and I felt very blessed to have actually seen his face. I don't know how many other people have actually seen God's face but I felt every fortunate at the time. It was truly a miracle!

My grandfather on my mother's side, Cove E. Stone, died on April 28, 1978. He had been hospitalized for a time when he aspirated into his lungs. I visited him every day at Holy Cross Hospital in Silver Spring and brought him his favorite newspaper, The Washington Post, to read. It is my favorite newspaper as well!

My grandfather came down from a long line of rabbi's in Poland, I was told by my parents. As a matter of fact, my father's father and mother's father came from the same town in Poland. The town was what was previously called Russia Poland but was incorporated into what is now Russia.

One night, in my haunted house, I saw a red, glowing ball about one foot in diameter approaching me below the ceiling of my bedroom. The ball was moving in a somewhat erratic motion towards me. I quickly closed my eyes since I was scared. This was definitely a paranormal experience and I was afraid to see what it was!

I was still visiting my grandfather at the hospital when, on one afternoon, I noticed that he did not finish his food. I informed his nurse that he did not finish his food and she began to feed him. Suddenly, he began to aspirate his food into his lungs.

When a nurse put a plastic tube into his throat to allow him to breathe, he bit the tube, showing that he wanted to die. He had contracted several infections while in the hospital which is very common and he felt very uncomfortable. Unfortunately, my grandfather died as I was holding his hand, urging him to breathe. I called my parents and they came to the hospital to see him one last time.

That evening, I felt very guilty at having the nurse continue to feed my grandfather. I felt that I was responsible for his death. I prayed to see my grandfather's face one last time.

Suddenly, on the ceiling of my room during the night, I actually saw his face in a gray, ghost-like apparition. His face was about twice the normal size. He had a smile on his face and his eyes were closed.

There was someone next to him whose face was also the same size. I felt that this was his guardian angel. I didn't recognize the face of his guardian angel since this was the first time I had seen him. I felt comforted at having seen my grandfather one more time since we were very close.

Several days later, the red ball appeared in my ceiling and was again coming towards me in the same, slow, erratic pattern. This time, I kept my eyes open. When the red ball arrived over my head, it changed suddenly into the shape of a large oval about three feet high and two feet wide. Three angels appeared in color with one male angel at the top of the oval and two female angels at the bottom of the oval.

All three angels were very young in appearance, looking about in their mid to late 20's. The male angel had blonde hair and one of the female angels also had blonde hair. The other female angel had brunette colored hair. All of the angels were white and simply looked at me as I looked at them. The female angels' hair were in braids, wrapped around the tops of their heads, appearing like women's hairdos during Roman times, several thousand years ago.

I wear glasses but all of the appearances by God and his angels at nighttime are always in focus and clear. I knew then that I was being comforted by God's angels after the passing of my grandfather and that I was not to blame for his death.

The angels had visited me prior to his death to alert me of his pending death but I was too afraid to open my eyes. They visited me after his death to let me know that God was always with me and my grandfather's spirit was with God in heaven.

Since I had left the U.S. Government in 1976 in order to run for U.S. Congress, I traveled around the world working on a special project for the Republic of China on Taiwan, the ROC, as the Taiwan government is known. This project entailed trying to encourage other governments to recognize the ROC through establishment of diplomatic relations.

In the early 1980's, only 24 countries recognized Taiwan diplomatically. Due to the presence of the People's Republic of China, otherwise known as the PRC, it was virtually a "mission impossible" to convince other governments to recognize the ROC. The PRC claims that the ROC is a "renegade province" of the PRC and most countries are reluctant to recognize the ROC due to the immense size and diplomatic power of the PRC.

In addition to the diplomatic relations project with the ROC, I was asked by Taiwan's CIA Director to obtain certain military items from the U.S. Government. This request needed to be staffed through numerous agencies of the U.S. Government. However, since the U.S. Government derecognized the ROC in 1979, this project was on a covert basis.

I just happened to be passing through Taipei, Taiwan, in 1979 when the U.S. Government derecognized Taiwan in favor of the PRC. There were demonstrations throughout Taipei by a very unhappy people. I, to this date, fail to recognize the benefit of this action by the U.S. Government since a "two China" recognition policy could have worked. However, the PRC refused to abide by the "two China" recognition and the U.S. caved in.

Prior to traveling to Taipei in the early 1980's, I had made arrangements with a U.S. intelligence operative for direct contact with him while I was in Taiwan. This was for my own protection since the mission was on a covert basis.

The code name for the mission was, "Class of '52 West Point Military Academy". The intelligence operative had dual credentials as it is known in the intelligence field. He held both CIA and FBI credentials and simply pulled out a credential which was specific for a particular mission. Our main contact with the U.S. Government was the Chairman of the Joint Chiefs of Staff at that time. The President was aware of the operation.

I travelled to Taipei with a Taiwanese associate of mine to meet certain individuals involved with military sales for Taiwan. I didn't know at the time that it was against the law to sell military items in Taiwan without specific authorization. Although I had been involved with the Taiwan government for years, there was a lapse in communication with a certain part of the ROC government apparently.

I even went to the office of the ROC CIA Director concerning the project. He himself was selling small arms to the U.S. military with his own munitions factory. In addition, he was supplying stainless steel parts to the U.S. Navy for their ships. One thing which I liked was the fact that he owned a bakery in his office building and we enjoyed excellent food and pastries during our meetings!

At one point during my trip, I was informed that we were breaking the law and may be arrested. However, when my name was referred by the Taiwan CIA through a "back channel" or covert contact with the U.S. Government, my mission was acknowledged by the Chairman of the Joint Chiefs of Staff personally.

When he was asked if he knew me, he replied, "Yes. He is a very good man!" This confirmation immediately gave me instant credentials with the ROC Government. It also gave me some relief since I was helping the ROC Government with their military requirements.

Upon arrival back in the U.S., I had arranged with my intelligence contact or "control" to meet with a representative of the ROC government regarding military items for purchase by the ROC from the U.S .government. The ROC representative was arriving at Washington National Airport and I was to meet him upon his arrival. I was told that we were all under surveillance by U.S. intelligence agents to be sure that everything went well.

Although I was somewhat nervous, the ROC representative met with the appropriate U.S. intelligence agents regarding the purchase of certain military items for the ROC. However, all they wanted to do was to copy some of our military items for their own use. This was unfortunate since a lot of time and effort was put into the project by many individuals.

One of my Taiwanese agents gave me some background information about the death of Bruce Lee. We all loved Bruce Lee in his kung fu movies since he was so fast, accurate and powerful.

My agent told me that she knew Bruce Lee's Taiwanese girlfriend and she was with him when he had died in Hong Kong. She stated that due to Bruce Lee's immense power, his activities in bed were too exhausting for him which may have contributed to his death.

His Taiwanese girlfriend fled Hong Kong since the police were looking for her as a possible suspect in his death. This account was according to my Taiwanese agent after Bruce Lee's girlfriend arrived back in Taiwan.

My intelligence operative was also involved with the Grenada operation in the early 1980's. I was told that the USSR was trying to take over Grenada using military personnel from Russia, Czechoslovakia, East Germany and other communist satellite countries.

Once they took over Grenada, the USSR planned to use Grenada as a "stepping stone" to take over all of Central and South America. I was also told that the USSR had excavated a submarine base under the island for the use of their cargo submarines. The USSR's cargo submarines were capable of transporting tanks and other large weapon systems.

The Prime Minister of Grenada, Sir Eric Gary, was visiting in the U.S. at that time when the USSR and its communist satellite operatives took over the country. They had taken over all of the radio stations and announced the takeover.

Sir Gary was knighted by the Queen of England. He was secreted in a CIA "safe house" in Arlington, Virginia at the time of the takeover. I was asked to come to the safe house to take part in a debriefing. At that time, it was not known what the future of Grenada may be.

The U.S. Government had formulated a plan to rescue Americans who were attending college in Grenada as the cover operation to push the communist military out of the country. Even though we lost a helicopter with its crew during the "rescue operation", the mission was a complete success. The USSR was defeated under the guise of rescuing Americans attending college. Fortunately, Grenada was able to withstand the grasp of the communists.

Also, during the early 1980's, I had traveled extensively to Jamaica. At that time, Prime Minister Edward Seaga was the leader of the country. His main opposition was the pro-communist Michael Manley. Again, my covert project of establishing diplomatic relations with the ROC was my objective. However, since the PRC had made significant inroads to the island, diplomatic relations with the ROC was not of interest to the government.

I had met Prime Minister Seaga during a fund raising event. He was educated in the U.S. and was very popular in Jamaica. When I arrived initially in the island, a nursing home had burned down with no help from the fire department which was very close by. The U.S. CIA was blamed for the fire by the PNP, People's National Party, of Michael Manley. The opposition party was the JLP, Jamaican Labor Party, of Edward Seaga.

Of course, the U.S. CIA never set the fire. The PNP of Michael Manley, being pro-communist, is alleged to have set the fire. Many senior citizens died in the fire. It was alleged that the communists have no use for senior citizens.

I had traveled over the island extensively in a small British passenger plane and by car as well. The island is quite beautiful. I went to a town called Clarendon which had numerous fields of sugar cane. The sugar cane was quite tall, towering well over my head!

I was especially fond of the Jamaican food including curry goat, lobster, ackee and cod fish, naseberry fruit and goat head soup called Mannish Water. Mannish Water gives you instant energy when you eat it. I watched the chef burning off the hair from the goat head and chopping it up into little pieces before cooking the head. The soup is made from the goat brains and is quite tasty.

I even tried the over proof rum which is 150 proof or 75% alcohol. When I first arrived in Jamaica at Montego Bay, my agent mixed some over proof rum with fresh fruit juices in a large blender. I drank a large glass of the mixture and, after awhile, felt sleepy. I lay down and was out for five hours! The rum had knocked me out!

I woke up at midnight to the crowing of a rooster since roosters crow at midnight in Jamaica instead of sunup in the U.S. At Montego Bay, I went down to the shore with my agent and met the lobster man with his lobster pot. He was selling fresh spiny lobsters for $6.00 each. The lobsters were very large and were simply delicious although they had no claws. I never eat lobster claws anyway so I was happy.

While eating the lobster, there were hot peppers called scotch bonnets. I actually thought that they were pieces of cauliflower since they resembled the vegetable. However, when I brought the scotch bonnet to my lips, there was an immediate burning sensation all down my throat. Fortunately I didn't eat the scotch bonnet since I would never have survived!

My first trip to the Philippines was in 1979, the same time that I traveled to Taiwan. Again, my trip was involved with establishing diplomatic relations with Taiwan. I had met the Philippine ambassador to the U.S., Ambassador Romualdez, who in turn referred me to the Minister of Energy in the Philippines.

Minister of Energy Velasco arrived at my Hyatt Hotel on Roxas Boulevard with his two bodyguards. I was given bodyguards as well even though I didn't feel the need to have them. At that time, there was a lot of shooting in the Philippines and security was of paramount concern to everyone.

I also met Vicente Romualdez, the older brother of the first lady, Imelda Marcos. Vicente was 72 years old when I met him and was a tall, charismatic gentleman. We struck up an immediate friendship and traveled around Manila to various restaurants, enjoying each other's company.

Vicente was the only Romualdez to decline the use of bodyguards. Unfortunately, diplomatic relations with Taiwan was not of interest to the Philippine government. Vicente later passed away in the U.S. and Imelda brought his body back to the Philippines for burial.

I had also met General Constante Ma.Cruz in the Philippines. President Marcos had appointed him as the Philippine representative to SEATO, Southeast Asia Treaty Organization. General Cruz was known as "Tante" for short and was a very likeable individual. Unfortunately, he had developed cancer and went to Pennsylvania to be with his relatives for treatment.

Over the phone prior to his passing, he told me, "John, my doctor is giving me progesterone injections and I am developing breasts!" I knew that this is one of the treatments for cancer and had hoped that it would work for him. However, he soon had passed away and I felt very sad for his family.

On one occasion while staying at the Inter-Continental Hotel in Manila, Tante had visited me even though he was very ill with the beginning of the cancer. His daughter later told me that he never visits anyone while being so ill but made an exception for me.

I felt very proud to have been visited by Tante in his seriously ill condition! In addition to being a Brigadier General in the Philippine Army, Tante was a former Assistant Minister of National Defense in the Philippine government.

I first traveled to Taiwan with one of my associates from the U.S. Department of Labor. We had intended to visit his contact who was an investigator with the Taiwan Ministry of Foreign Affairs located at Taichung, the provincial capital of Taiwan. However, his contact was too busy to meet with us since he was on an active investigation with the ministry and could not leave his post.

We were given housing at the Chiang Kai-shek's villa in Taichung and were honored to have stayed there for several days. Close by the villa we heard what sounded like women screaming. When we asked our escort what the noise was, he replied that it was due to caged peacocks!

Sure enough, when he brought us to a caged enclosure close by the villa, we saw hundreds of peacocks who were emitting a strange sound like screaming women. It was definitely surrealistic and hard to believe that peacocks could make such strange sounds.

I would later learn that Madame Chiang Kai-shek was involved with covert operations with the Republic of Taiwan while living in New York. One of my Taiwanese intelligence contacts informed me that she was involved with so-called, "black bag", operations involving military sales for Taiwan. Such operations required moving large amounts of money destined for Taiwan's military requirements.

In the early 1980's, Pan American Airlines had offered a special airfare for around the world trips. The cost was $999.00. I availed myself of this outstanding airfare and traveled around the world several times visiting numerous countries in Asia and Europe. As long as you travel in one direction, the trip was allowed. I even was able to make "delay on routes" to stop over at a country I wanted to visit with no problem.

During one of my trips to London in the early 1980's I met a colleague who was involved with Swiss Franc conversions to U.S. dollars. He was working with very large European banks for the transactions involving hundreds of millions of dollars. Unfortunately, the bank officers made the transaction themselves, according to my colleague, and cut everybody involved out of the transaction so that they alone could profit.

When I returned to the U.S., I continued to work with my colleague with Swiss Franc conversions and made contact with Juanita Poitier, the first wife of actor Sidney Poitier. I spoke with Juanita on several occasions and learned that she resided in Long Island, New York.

I also made contact with Joseph Jackson, the father of Michael Jackson, regarding Swiss Franc conversions as well. When I spoke with Joseph Jackson who was living in California, I asked him," Are you the father of Michael Jackson?" Joseph replied to me, "I am the father of all of the Jacksons!"

Michael Jackson and I shared the same birthday of August 29th! Unfortunately, I was not successful in any Swiss Franc conversion transactions since they were in the "mission impossible" realm.

Using the Pan American Airlines special around the world ticket, I traveled to West Africa visiting Ghana, Nigeria, Gambia and Sierra Leone. . I traveled extensively around Ghana since I had a contact with the Special Branch, an intelligence section of the government.

When I arrived in Accra in 1980, I did not have a visa since my travel agent in Maryland informed me that a visa was not required. When I entered the airport immigration area, I was asked for my visa. I stated that I was told that a visa was not required.

Just then, a tall man asked me if I was Mr. Seiden. I replied in the affirmative and he asked me to accompany him. I went with him to a small office where I paid $5.00 for a visa. The person with me was a member of the Special Branch who was waiting for my arrival.

Unfortunately, Ghana was not interested in diplomatic relations with Taiwan. However, I did enjoy my two trips to Ghana in 1980 and 1981. I especially enjoyed the food: curry goat, peanut soup, cocoa yams, fried plantains, fufu, kenkey, papaya and Club beer. I even learned some of the Twi tribal language.

One of the Special Branch agents asked for my help to leave Ghana. Since he was in charge of airport security for Kotoka International Airport in Accra, Ghana, he just could not leave the country without authorization. He asked for my assistance in obtaining a visa for Hong Kong.

I brought him to the British Embassy in Accra where he applied for a visa and was approved for himself and his girlfriend. When I was to leave Ghana, he asked me to proceed with him out of the airport terminal. He gave his jacket to one person, his suitcase to another and his necktie to still another person to hide his departure. When on the plane, he celebrated his "escape" from the country.

I have traveled extensively to China over the years. During a visit to Canton with my Chinese agent, we went to a Chinese Army compound to fire AK47 assault rifles. I had never fired an AK47 during my military service and looked forward to firing the weapon.

David was with me and we both fired the AK47. We both fired the weapon in the prone position with ear protection. I forgot to tell David to hold the weapon tight to his shoulder and he suffered a black and blue mark accordingly.

I paid one of the Chinese Army officers $100 for the ammunition since he had a little business on the side, apparently. The weapon was beautifully designed with a blond wooden stock. When it fired, a loud "boom" occurred, much louder than U.S. Army weapons.

I knew that the AK47 is practically indestructible and can be dropped in water, snow, mud, etc., and function normally. I even loaded the round canisters used to hold the rifle shells along with the Chinese military personnel. I later spoke with someone who said that the loud boom was designed to scare enemy combatants. This makes sense since the boom scared me as well!

During the same trip, we went to a Chinese restaurant on the military compound. The restaurant was famous for its snake menu. We went to the top of the restaurant to peer down to the snake pit and saw numerous snakes moving about.

The snakes were broiled and brought to the table in a small brown crucible. They tasted good but had too many tiny bones. However, I also ate pieces of snake which were deep fried with honey and sesame seeds brought to the table on chopsticks mounted horizontally. The snake was chewy and simply delicious!

My Chinese agent was actually born in Macao but held both a Hong Kong permit plus a British passport. I have known him for many years, having met him when he was Deputy Managing Director of Kingley

Commodities in Hong Kong, a precious metals firm. I was introduced to him through the family of President Marcos of the Philippines who owned the company.

My Chinese agent told me that he once dated the neice of the last emperor of China. Her name was Ai Seen Jhou Lau, Seong Ting. I was very impressed at this piece of information since who could claim to have dated a royal figure, especially in China!

On another trip, I traveled to Shanghai with several of my associates. The city was simply beautiful, just like downtown New York. There was even a sign downtown which read, "Times Square". We even went to the TV Tower, an immense structure which towered over several rivers below.

We had the opportunity to go to the town of Pudong where I again ate snake. This time, since it was my turn to pay for dinner, I ordered a $40 snake as part of the dinner menu. The snake was very large and was deep fried. It was simply exquisite!

To this day, I have not had the opportunity to eat snake again. During the same dinner party with my associates, we also ate lotus blossom roots. The roots were simply delicious and tasted like potatoes but with a richer flavor. The roots were simply immense!

During the same visit to Pudong, I went to a small specialty restaurant which served exotic food. This time I ate a large piece of corned donkey beef. It was just like corned beef you would get in the U.S. The beef was very tasty and I didn't even go, "hee-haw" afterwards.

We were traveling in a Chinese General's staff car at the time and had the complete right-of-way on all of the roads. It was nice to be able to travel anywhere we wanted to go with no restrictions. This could never happen in the U.S. on our highways since we had to follow the rules of the road. But in China if you are with a V.I.P., anything goes, obviously.

I had met the presidential candidate for Ecuador, Lucio Gutierrez, in Georgetown, Washington, D.C. in 2002. I also met his wife, a beautiful redhead, at the same time along with my Ecuadorian associate.

Mr. Gutierrez knew that I was involved with Taiwan for my recognition project and asked for funds for his campaign. When I submitted his request to the ROC, it was flatly turned down. The ROC stated that he would have to become President first before any financial assistance could be given to Ecuador.

I traveled soon thereafter to Ecuador to meet my Ecuadorian associate after Mr. Gutierrez became President of Ecuador. We met with his Chief of Staff on the Taiwan project but were unable to accomplish our mission. The Chief of Staff was in a palace with guards posted outside in uniforms reminiscent of 16th century Spain. The uniforms were very colorful and the guards held lances.

During my visit to Ecuador, I was able to travel to Ambato, a very pleasant town with a hot spring outside. We went into the hot spring for a refreshing swim. During our trip around Ambato and Quito, the capital, we were accompanied by an armed guard of the military for safekeeping. I didn't feel that this was necessary but was in no position to question the decision.

While in Ambato, we went to an excellent restaurant where we had various cuts of meat such as roast beef and steak. The prices were astounding; only $1.75 for a steak dinner. In Quito, the capitol, such a dinner would cost four or five times as much.

I went to several restaurants in Quito and had a very delicious soup made out of potatoes. I also had a delicious chocolate cocoa drink. Cocoa is grown in Ecuador and, since I love chocolate, I was very happy to be able to drink the cocoa.

Quito was about 10,000 to 12,000 feet above sea level and it took me two weeks to adjust to the altitude since I had a hard time breathing. Once I adjusted after two weeks, I went home.

Ecuador is a very beautiful country and I hope to travel there again someday. After I left Ecuador, the country, "dollarized", which meant that the country adopted the dollar for their currency and prices immediately shot up.

In March 1990, I was driving my Le Mans Pontiac from my new apartment in Gaithersburg, Maryland, to my U.S. Government office in Washington, D.C. I was working the night shift from 10:00 p.m. to 6:00 a.m. A light snow was falling and I was driving in the fast lane at a high rate of speed when my car hydroplaned and spun 180 degrees around, striking a concrete lane divider. My car was then propelled into the middle lane of traffic and was struck by a tractor trailer, propelling me against the concrete lane divider before coming to rest pointing north in the southbound Route 270.

Three collisions in a matter of seconds. I was somewhat dizzy and bleeding from my left forehead and immediately got out of my car to get a roll of paper towels in the trunk to absorb the blood. Soon thereafter, an ambulance came to my rescue and brought me to the Shady Grove Adventist Hospital in Gaithersburg for treatment. I was placed in a neck brace and strapped in a stretcher before being placed in the ambulance. This was more uncomfortable than the injury I sustained!

I was x-rayed and examined by the hospital emergency room staff. I had received a mild concussion compounded by a bad gash to my left forehead which required 25 stitches. I was told that my doctor was the best in sewing stitches in the entire Washington, D.C. area. While he was sewing up my forehead, he said, "I love to sew, I love to sew". I was glad that he loved to sew since sewing the skin is a real art!

Just then, a police officer appeared in the emergency room where I was being attended by the physician. The police officer told me, "I am sorry to say that you were driving too fast for conditions and I have to give you a ticket. Please sign here".

Of course, I immediately signed the ticket since I knew that I was driving too fast in the light snow with an evident loss of traction. In addition, the police officer stated, "You know, you could have been killed if there was anyone behind you! I found your glasses 1/4th mile away from the collision." I guess I was really lucky; especially with my glasses being found by the police officer.

After being released from the hospital, I took a taxi back to my apartment. My family was shocked at my accident after seeing the stitches on my forehead. A few weeks later, I visited my car at a storage facility and was amazed to see that the Le Mans Pontiac was now a compact with deep dents on all sides with the top of the car smashed downward, contributing to my concussion.

The car was a total loss, of course, but I survived. That was all that mattered. I recovered quickly from the accident and returned to work after two weeks. I now know that God and my guardian angel were watching over me.

I was driving my 1990 Chevrolet Caprice on Maryland's 495 Beltway in July 1995. The weather was warm and sunny and I had opened both front windows. I felt sleepy and started to doze off while driving my car.

Suddenly, I saw something coming at me from my left rear, using my peripheral vision. It was a small, black polished oblong rock that glanced off my left cheek in a gentle manner before coming to rest on the passenger seat next to me.

The act of the rock touching my left cheek softly probably saved my life since I would have crashed into another vehicle. I felt that this was an act of God and was very happy to have His intervention.

I saved the rock since I felt it was holy. The rock immediately woke me up from my slumber and I was fully alert on my way home. I know now that my guardian angel was taking care of me as well and was thankful for her intervention!

I returned to the U.S. Government in 1985, having been out of the U.S. Government for nine years. I bought our new house in 1990 since it was just perfect to my family's needs and was close to my parent's home as well. I was continuing to pray every night and even during the day for my family.

I met Josie in Los Angeles, California in 2000. After a one year's engagement with my traveling back and forth from Maryland to California, we decided to get married. We were married on June 23, 2001, in Hotel Del Coronado, in Coronado, California, near the San Diego Naval Base. The marriage was officiated by both a Jewish rabbi and a Catholic priest since I am Jewish and Josie is Catholic. The marriage ceremony was conducted outside of the hotel by the beach.

The weather was very hot and I sustained a sunburn on my face. The wedding was beautiful and all of our families and relatives attended. We all had a great time with excellent food and a dance band.

During the evening in our hotel room, I was awakened five times by people talking, glasses clinking, and music. Josie was sleeping soundly but I was getting more and more irritated at the noise all during the night.

I remember seeing a sign at the upper level of the hotel where we were staying which said, "No parties after 10:00 pm". I couldn't believe that other residents in the hotel were having a party, making a lot of noise against the hotel's regulations!

At the last time I was awakened, I heard someone trying to open our room door with a key. I got up and almost headed downstairs from our penthouse room to confront the intruder when I suddenly remembered that we didn't use a key to our room but used a credit card style room key instead. This realization stopped me dead in my tracks. I knew then that something was amiss!

After we left the hotel, I learned that the hotel had ghosts! It was built in the 1860's and had a reputation for ghostly encounters. Since I had a lot of experience witnessing ghosts in my haunted house, I guess that I was very receptive to paranormal happenings.

Staying in a haunted hotel during my wedding was really an eye opener! If I were informed of the hotel's haunted background, I would not have believed its reputation. However, in my case, hearing is believing!

Two weeks after we were married, I traveled to Sierra Leone in West Africa again on my diplomatic recognition of Taiwan project. I flew from Baltimore-Washington International Airport along with my agent from Sierra Leone to Brussels, Belgium on Sabena Airlines. From Brussels we flew to Gambia, West Africa. From Gambia, we rode a large transport helicopter manned by Russian pilots.

The helicopter was very noisy on our 45 minute trip to Freetown, Sierra Leone. I stayed in Cape Sierra Hotel during the ten days that I was in Sierra Leone. The hotel had no hot water but the housekeepers brought hot water in a bucket to use for bathing.

The food was very good at the hotel restaurants in both Sierra Leone and Gambia. I especially enjoyed barracuda fish fillets, the best fish that I have ever eaten!

I really didn't know that the war was still going on in Sierra Leone. When I arrived at Cape Sierra Hotel, there was a British machine gun emplacement in front of the hotel. Throughout the city were bombed out buildings due to the war.

I went to an amputee camp in downtown Freetown where I saw men, women and children who had lost their limbs due to the rebels using machetes to cut them off. It was very sad, indeed, to have witnessed such atrocities.

I was told that the rebels had cut off peoples' heads and mounted them on cars. Also, I was told that rebels had accosted pregnant women and made a bet whether the fetus was male or female. They then cut out the fetus, killing both the mother and fetus to see who won the bet. The rebels were really horrible and committed unimaginable atrocities throughout the war!

I heard that the rebel leader was caught by the British and housed in a secret location. The rebels were heavily involved in the trading of the so-called "blood diamonds" which were mined and sold to finance their military activities.

The rebels used the term, "short sleeve", to denote the act of cutting off someone's arm and the term, "long sleeve", to denote cutting off someone's hand. The rebels were simply brutal in their actions and deserved to be punished accordingly!

I met the President's Senior Advisor, Dr. Sama Banya, at his home to discuss my Taiwan recognition project. He indicated that Sierra Leone was favorably disposed towards establishing diplomatic relations with Taiwan. However, nothing ever came of the diplomatic relations gambit for Sierra Leone. I returned back to the U.S., relieved that I survived a trip to a warn-torn country!

Soon after I returned from Sierra Leone in the summer of 2001, Josie, Justin our son and myself visited the World Trade Center in New York. It was simply a grand building with so much inside including vast amounts of restaurants, stores and offices.

We had gone on a sightseeing trip beforehand to New York Harbor with a swing by the Statue of Liberty. We took a stretch limousine from the harbor to the World Trade Center and simply had a great time.

Little did we know that on September 11, 2001, the building would simply collapse from the terrorist attack. Josie's mother called us on that morning to tell us to turn on the television. We immediately turned on the television and saw the two airplanes crashing into the building. It was simply heartbreaking and horrible at the same time!

Later we would learn that the terrorists received training in how to fly airplanes with no questions asked from the aviation school. Not only did the terrorists crash into the Twin Towers of the World Trade Center but they crashed into the Pentagon and on United Airlines Flight 93 in Shanksville, Pennsylvania when the passengers overpowered the terrorists. The passengers were very brave to overpower the terrorists in what would be their last day alive!

In the summer of 2007, Josie became pregnant with twins. We were simply ecstatic, knowing that we will have two more additions to our family with two beautiful daughters.

When Josie had her ultrasound at Holy Cross Hospital in Silver Spring, the procedure showed one blip which meant one baby. The following week she had another ultrasound which showed a second blip which meant she was going to have twins. We were simply astonished and overjoyed at the same time. We later learned that the twins were both female and we were very happy to have not one but two babies.

A few days before Josie gave birth, I saw a hoop above my head with red and green lights moving around its own axis. The hoop was about four to five feet in diameter. I just could not believe my own eyes. It was like a hula hoop from the 60's and it was truly a miracle.

The hoop appeared for about 15 to 20 seconds. I believe that the presence of the hoop was a way for God to prophesy the birth of our children, Jasmine and Jessica. A few days later, after the birth of our children, I noticed a circle of diamonds around my left eye, moving on its own axis like the hoop I previously encountered.

I thought that something was wrong with my left eye and immediately went downstairs to the bathroom to look into the mirror. I didn't see anything wrong with my left eye. The circle of diamonds lasted for several minutes. This was truly another miracle. I believe that God was showing his happiness at the birth of our children. In later years, the circle of diamonds appeared on several occasions during an important event. I never questioned the appearance of the circle of diamonds since I felt that they were holy in nature.

Our twins were born 10 weeks prematurely. Jasmine was 3 pounds and 8 ounces and Jessica weighed 2 pounds and 9 ounces. Jasmine remained in the Neonatal Intensive Care Unit (termed NICU Unit) for five weeks and Jessica remained in the NICU Unit for six weeks, due to their being born premature, at Holy Cross Hospital in Silver Spring, Maryland.

Josie and I visited them every day since they were born on December 5, 2007, a snowy day. Both girls had excellent medical care at the hospital, one of the best hospitals in the Washington, D.C. area. I was told that the NICU Unit was the best in the area as well. The doctors and nurses at Holy Cross Hospital were all superb and our twins have grown into beautiful, young, healthy girls.

Since I like to bake desserts, I baked a double batch of brownies with walnuts and chocolate chip every week for the medical staff. Everyone loved my brownies and I was very happy to bake for all of the doctors and nurses to show my appreciation for taking care of Jasmine and Jessica around the clock for the entire period of their stay in the hospital.

Someone suggested that I should open a bakery since my brownies were so popular. However, I just like to bake for a hobby and everyone's enjoyment as well. I have thought about opening a bakery over the years. However, I knew that if you have a bakery or another type of store that you need to be away from the family most of the time. I could never do that since the family, to me, is more important!

About a week after the birth of our two beautiful twins, another miracle occurred. During the night, a cherub appeared above me in color. It was a beautiful baby angel with a fat face who closely resembled Jasmine. The angel was holding a wand and was moving it back and forth like a metronome on top of a piano. On the back of the angel was a set of small, white wings. I was really astonished at having seen the cherub and was delighted as well.

The angel was smiling widely and seemed to be communicating with me its happiness at the birth of our children. I couldn't tell whether the cherub was a male or a female since it was a baby about one to one and one-half years old.

The cherub appeared for about ten to fifteen seconds and then disappeared. The very next night, I prayed to see the cherub once more. From the left corner of my room, I saw the cherub's hand waving to me. The hand was by itself and appeared for only a few seconds

Both the cherub and its hand were in color and were in perfect focus. Anything I see at night is automatically adjusted to compensate for my being near-sighted. This is in itself a miracle since I don't wear my glasses at night, of course!

I am convinced that Jasmine saw the same cherub a few weeks later when I was feeding her and putting her to sleep at about 1:30 p.m. During her feeding time, she was waving very hard at someone behind me. When I looked back, I didn't see anything.

The very next day, the same situation repeated itself. Jasmine waved very hard at someone behind me. Again, when I looked behind me, there was nothing there. The waving by Jasmine never repeated itself since that time.

I have had numerous instances of God's presence both in and around my home. Once, when I was outside at the back of my home walking down from my porch, I felt a hand across my back along with an outstretched arm. I looked back but didn't see anyone behind me. I felt that this was the hand of God comforting me.

Also, when I was walking down the stairs at the back of my home, suddenly I was thrown into the air and landed on the grass, unhurt, onto my right side. I didn't know how this could have happened since I didn't trip coming down the stairs at all. To this day, I don't know what triggered this event to happen but just feel that it was a holy occasion showing the power of God!

At a certain time, I felt that God had left me and was feeling somewhat disillusioned during the night time. All of a sudden, someone struck the middle toe of my right foot, causing some pain.

Since I was in the habit of wearing socks at night during the winter under a heavy comforter, I was alarmed how this could happen. I realized then that God never left me and wanted to remind me of this fact. I also realized that God did not want me to harbor such thoughts. Since that time, my love for God has been steadfast.

During most every evening between 1:00 a.m. and 4:00 a.m., I am visited by numerous angels. The angels present themselves by various forms of light either in circles, flashes or faces. Sometimes the faces are in color and sometimes they are in black and white. At times, the faces are beautiful and other times they are very scary looking. This has been going on for many years in all of my homes as well as during my overseas trips.

On one occasion during the middle of the night, I was praying to God when I saw a large group of people in color who were completely nude from the waist up, both men and women. They were composed of young beautiful women and young handsome men, all white. I believe that they were all angels from heaven above. They were all smiling and mingling together and looking down upon me.

It felt very warm and comforting to see all of these angels looking down upon me from my ceiling above. I only saw the group of angels once and will never forget them. It was as if these angels were showing their love for me since I felt their love and affection in their demeanor towards me by their smiling faces and warm movements.

Josie and I have been driving our son, Justin, to his high school every morning. We took turns in driving him to school. Since I didn't set my alarm clock to wake up in the morning, I had the habit of looking at the clock every few hours to see the time. I prayed to God that He or one of His angels could wake me up between 5:45 a.m. and 6:00 a.m. since Justin had to be at school by 7:25 a.m.

On one occasion in May of 2010, I was awakened by someone snapping the back of my underpants at 5:45 a.m. Apparently, one of God's angels put her fingers inside the back of my underpants and simply pulled the elastic of the underpants back and let it go. What a wake-up call that was!

This was especially surprising since the angel put her hand through my comforter on top of my body with no sound. This only happened one time but it really made me realize that God and His angels are always around us and always respond to our prayers, no matter what they may be.

I then realized that this was my guardian angel and she had responded to my prayer to God that I be awakened to drive Justin to school on time. I have given the name of Divine to my guardian angel since she is holy.

The very next day, I was sleeping and during the early morning hours, someone had poked their finger at my right index finger. I was alarmed, of course, but felt that my guardian angel was trying to get my attention. She really got my attention since this was the second time that there was direct contact between my guardian angel and myself!

On November 3, 2009, my father, Jacob Seiden, passed away one week before his 99th birthday. He was born on November 10, 1910, in New York City. He told me that he grew up knowing the famous comedian Sid Caesar in New York. Both of my parents met Frank Sinatra in Beverly Hills, California years ago.

My father's brother-in-law was Dave Barry, a famous comedian as well. I had met Uncle Dave, as I called him of course, when I was very young, perhaps 10 or 11 years old. Uncle Dave used to perform on the Ed Sullivan Show in the 1950's on live television.

I remember him performing during intermission in a movie theater when I was very young, perhaps about nine or ten. During one of his intermission performances, he held a green flashlight in one hand and a red flashlight in another, during the dark, pretending that he was an airplane coming in for a landing. Uncle Dave had made an LP record with his comedy routines as well.

One of my aunts was an official with the AFL-CIO. During one of her meetings in the Shoreham Hotel in Washington, D.C. in the 1980's, she had invited the famous comedian Danny Kaye to perform for a few minutes. After his performance, I followed him out of the hotel to shake his hand. I had to run after him to shake his hand since he was walking so fast. I think that he was trying to avoid the crowd but I was determined to shake his hand and accomplished the mission!

I remember when I was a little boy and my father used to read me the 23rd Psalm from the Old Testament when I was in bed before I went to sleep:

> The Lord is my Shepherd; I shall not want.
>
> He maketh me to lie down in green pastures;
>
> He leadeth me beside the still waters,
>
> He restoreth my soul;
>
> He leadeth me in the paths of righteousness for His name' sake.
>
> Yea, though I walk through the valley of the shadow of death,
>
> I will fear no evil;
>
> For thou art with me;
>
> Thy rod and thy staff, they comfort me.
>
> Thou preparest a table before me in the presence of mine enemies;
>
> Thou annointest my head with oil;
>
> My cup runneth over.
>
> Surely goodness and mercy shall follow me all the days of my life,
>
> And I will dwell in the House of the Lord forever.

I felt comforted when my father read me the 23rd Psalm from the Old Testament of the bible. I felt a very strong connection with God at an early age because of my father.

About one month before my father's passing, I felt a very warm and comforting presence on my back during the evening hours. This presence lasted for two days. During the middle of the second day in the night, I saw a spirit leave my body and go upwards. The spirit was very large and thick with an elongated head at the very end.

The spirit was larger than my own body. Since I pray every night, "Now I lay me down to sleep, I pray the Lord my soul to keep and if I should die before I wake, I pray the Lord my soul to take", I thought that I was seeing my soul going to heaven for safekeeping. However, an angel's voice whispered in my left ear one word, "God". The voice was a woman's voice and it was the only time I have ever heard a voice from an angel.

I was at that moment taken aback and shocked at the same time! It was God's own Holy Spirit that was with me for two nights to comfort me prior to the passing of my father. I realized later that my guardian angel had whispered in my ear the presence of God's Holy Spirit that evening.

God, obviously, can see the future and knew that my father would die soon. Obviously, then, God can see the future, present and past. In addition, God and His angels can read your mind at all times and know what you are thinking at all times as well. This is somewhat unnerving and scary as well, knowing that God and His angels know what you are thinking, planning to do, etc. Of course, God and His angels can do anything they want to do at all times. This is what makes Him so powerful and so all knowing since the beginning of time and lasting forever. God has made the entire solar system and life everywhere and He knows all that was, all that is and all that will be.

Several months after my father's passing, I saw his ghost during the evening. I have seen a ghost before in my haunted house and immediately recognized the apparition. While I have no conclusive evidence that it was my father, I felt that it was him since the ghost was about his size.

The ghost was about five feet tall and about three feet wide. His spirit appeared inside a gray apparition in color. There was a blurry color of an individual inside the ghost and a gray outer appearance just like at the haunted house. The ghost was moving somewhat up and down, hovering if you might say, for about five to ten seconds before disappearing. I just felt that it was my father's ghost visiting me and I felt comforted at the sight and visitation.

While in my home office one afternoon about a month after my father's passing, I was looking for the schedule of my mother's housekeepers and nurse. I found the schedule under some other papers and retrieved it only to find a large drop of water on top of the schedule.

I was amazed to find the large drop of water since there was no water leaking from the ceiling and anyway, the schedule was not out in the open. During the next evening, I saw a pitcher of water at the upper left portion of my ceiling and a glass of water at the upper right portion of my ceiling. I immediately felt that God had shed a tear for the passing of my father. The appearance of the pitcher of water and glass of water the very next evening served to reinforce this feeling of mine. There is no other explanation that makes sense to me.

Several months after my father's passing, I received many signs from God, all physical in nature. It first started when I was sitting on my sofa and there began a tapping on my head. First, there was a gentle tap on the back of my head for several days. Then a series of four or five taps on the top of my head. I thought that I was imagining the taps but after three or four times I began to feel that God was encouraging me to begin writing.

There were other signs that were apparently from God. For example, when I went outside to get my daily newspaper and I was about to open the front door on the way back, the metal mail latch which was previously used for mail deliveries, opened and closed by itself. I thought that one of my two twins was playing games with me. However, when I opened the door, I found both children at the opposite end of the room. There was no way that they could have opened the spring-mounted latch from their position in the room. I now know that the opening of the latch was due to my guardian Angel. She wanted me to know of her presence since she is always with me no matter where I go!

On another occasion, I went outside to check on the weather and saw some clouds in the sky. When I was about to come inside the house by the front steps, about 50 to 75 rain drops fell on top of me. I looked around to see if it was raining but there was no rain in sight, only on top of me. I looked at the ground around me and saw a scattering of rain drops and quickly realized that they were heaven sent.

The next day, when my family and I were inside our living room, we heard a series of tapping on the bedroom wall adjacent to our living room. I said to my wife, Josie, "What was that?" She was as alarmed as I was and had no explanation for the tapping. I knew at that time that the tapping was holy in nature but didn't want to upset Josie. I later surmised that the tapping was from my guardian angel who was trying to get our attention to let us know that she is always around us.

It was at 8:30 a.m. on a Saturday morning, May 15, 2010, I had just opened my eyes and saw a smiling face looking down at me. The face was gray in appearance and the individual smiling at me seemed to be surprised and taken aback when I looked up at him since he probably wasn't expecting me to wake up so suddenly and immediately look at him.

Whomever it was – God, my father or an angel, suddenly had a very large grin and showed a large mouth full of teeth. In addition, he head was like a skull, devoid of hair or skin. The individual appeared to be an older man but I really didn't recognize him. The apparition lasted only a few seconds and disappeared by moving upward at a right angle very quickly.

Rarely have I ever been visited by God, His angels or a ghost during the daylight hours. Whenever I have a visitation it is normally late at night or during the early hours of the next day. I consider myself to be very blessed to have been visited by a spiritual entity or apparition during the morning hours. It was very unusual indeed and a little bit scary to say the least! I later surmised that it may have been my father's spirit, watching over me.

Josie had bad news in May of 2010. Her older brother, Ernie, had suffered a second stroke due to smoking and was paralyzed on his left side. He had numerous blood clots in his brain and heart as well and was not expected to live. We had not visited the Philippines since 2003 and didn't plan on going there until 2011 to renew our wedding vows in a special ceremony. We needed to visit Ernie in the hospital before it was too late! Therefore, we planned a 10 day trip to Manila commencing on May 20th until June 1st of 2010.

A few days prior to our departure, I was frantically searching for a file which one of my clients requested. I searched everywhere both upstairs and downstairs in numerous cabinets and storage boxes. However, I just couldn't find the missing file. When all seemed lost, I looked on top of a file cabinet on which I had placed a few files. When I picked up the files, I was shocked to find the missing file along with another file that I was recently searching for. The missing file just appeared "out of the blue." It was definitely not there previously since I had checked the top of the file cabinet several times.

I know that God or one of His angels had intervened on my behalf and placed the missing file along with the other file on top of the cabinet for me. This reminded me years ago when a card in my card file just popped up by itself when I was trying to find it. Both events were miracles in themselves since I was actively searching for items but could not locate them by myself.

Clearly, God and His angels can read your mind at all times and can help solve your urgent problems immediately! Now I know that my guardian Angel, Divine, had found the missing files for me and was very happy to have her with me and take care of me continually!

On another occasion prior to our trip, I was going down the back stairs of our porch and looked backwards through the steps. To my astonishment, a plant was being shaken furiously between several other plants. There was no wind at all at that time and I was startled at the plant being shaken by itself. It was as if someone was holding the plant and shaking it at me. I knew that God or one of His angels was trying to get my attention and succeeded! I later surmised that my guardian angel, Divine, was shaking the plant.

While on the airplane going to the Philippines at 37,000 feet, I was sitting on an aisle seat when someone brushed against my left arm. There was no one in the area at all since I checked in both directions. I was surprised at God's or His angel's presence at 37,000 feet having made contact with me at that location. However, since God and His angels are able to do anything, anywhere, I wasn't that surprised. I know now that my guardian angel, Divine, had brushed against my left arm to let me know that she was always with me, no matter where I was.

On June 9, 2010, we went to California for a scheduled two-week vacation. As usual, I prayed during the evening hours for my family. I didn't see any evidence of angels on my ceiling of the room in which we were staying in my sister-in-law's home in Santa Clarita. I wondered if the angels were still around and what happened to them since I always have a daily visitation of the angels.

Just then, an arm appeared in color at the left side of the room at eye level. The arm was pointing to the ceiling as if to remind me that angels are always around me. I was a little scared but greatly relieved that the angels were always with me. I will never have any doubt that God and His angels are always with me at all times.

When we came back from our trip, I was praying during the middle of the morning when a hand appeared at the right side of my bed with a long stem red rose. I was very delighted at seeing this since I felt that God and His angels were showing their love to my family and myself.

I have a photographic memory! For example, I can remember when I was in diapers in my home in Seattle and I was walking downstairs when I pooped in my pants, to put it mildly. I was walking with a "load" in my pants and it felt very heavy, of course.

On another occasion, I remember trying to talk to my brother to ask him where our mother was. I was not able to talk at that time, being about one year old or less.

However, I remember that gibberish came out of my mouth but my brother knew what I was trying to say and told me that our mother was next door with a neighbor. I was greatly relieved, of course, to hear where she was.

On another occasion when I was about one or one and one-half, my father was taking a picture of both my brother and myself next to each other and I was always falling over. I had to be repositioned several times to be photographed together. On another occasion, I explicitly remember climbing up to my high chair to eat a meal. I must have been about one and one half or two years of age at that time.

I was born in Springfield, Ohio on August 29, 1943. When I was about 1 or 2 years old, I remember a serious event which had occurred at Wright Patterson Air Force Base where we were living. My father was an officer in the old Army Air Corps at the time.

Someone was injured in a laboratory when an explosion had occurred and ran out of the building. This was a very scary event since my father was very alarmed and I could hear fire engines and ambulances with their sirens in the area. My brother and I both ran to hide behind our beds since we were so scared!

I can remember most things of importance to me exactly as they occur with a picture in my mind of the event. Thus, I am able to recall a picture of any scene which occurred such as God's face, an angel or a cherub at any time.

In Seattle, one day, I was riding my bike down the middle of the street with no hands, trying to be somewhat macho as children do at times. Suddenly, I lost control and the bike locked up, flipping me over the handlebars. I landed in the middle of the street. Several cars stopped to see if I was injured.

Fortunately, I didn't even have a scratch from the accident, not even a bruise. I know now that God and my guardian angel were watching over me and prevented me from sustaining any harm. I was seven or eight years old at the time.

In Wheaton, Maryland, when I was 12 or 13, I was coming out of a store near our apartments when I walked into an alley where cars occasionally drive. A car hit me as I was walking and I fell down.

Again, luckily, I was not hurt. The driver of the car got out to see if I was injured and I told him that I was okay. This was evidence that God and my guardian angel were watching over me and I feel very proud and blessed with His constant care of me and my guardian angel as well.

On August 7, 2010, we went to a seafood restaurant and had a lot of food to eat. This would not be so bad for me only I ate an excellent piece of chocolate cake and had some ice cream as well; a recipe for disaster. I had my usual acid blocker pill early in the evening but had to use an antacid treatment five or six times during the night to prevent my usual acid reflux from occurring.

After feeding Jessica, I placed her baby bottle on my right side before going to sleep. I got up five or six times during the night to drink my antacid and threw the covers over the baby bottle.

When I got up in the morning, I looked for the baby bottle next to me or on the floor where it should have been. I didn't see the bottle at all. However, when I walked towards the door, I saw the bottle neatly placed on the other side of the bed. I knew that my guardian angel had placed the bottle there since it would have fallen to the floor from the numerous times I had thrown back the covers. I was astounded at this happening and pleasantly surprised as well since it showed the love of my guardian angel for myself and my daughter.

Before I go to bed, I always place my glasses on the nightstand adjacent to my bed. Upon awakening in the morning, one day, my glasses were nowhere to be found. I looked everywhere but just could not find them.

I looked under the bed and lo and behold, I found my glasses neatly folded! I never fold my glasses before going to bed and, of course, would never place them under my bed. I realized then that my guardian angel had placed my glasses under my bed to play a trick on me.

She is sometimes very playful and I appreciated her attention which she showed me. The disappearance of my glasses never happened again. However, recently I noticed that my phone charger was unplugged. I asked Josie, Jasmine and Jessica if either of them had unplugged my charger. They all denied unplugging my charger and I, therefore, concluded that Divine had unplugged it in her playful mood. I was, of course, amused at her playfulness and appreciated her constant attention!

On September 15, 2010, I was praying during the early morning hours to see some angels once again since it has been awhile since I have seen them. Suddenly, I saw a red glow coming towards me with some faces in color which appeared to be angels. A hand appeared in front of me with what looked like a stick or rolled up paper and swiped across my face with an angry move, I thought. Since my mother was 90 years old, I thought that I might be seeing an advance notification of her nearing death.

However, this scene of the anger from an angel quickly dispelled this thought. I felt somewhat embarrassed at my thinking about my mother's imminent passing since she was still in good health. I was wrong, obviously, for looking for a sign of my mother's passing and this was probably why the angel acted in this manner.

I saw God's face in my old haunted house in 1982. At that time, His face was gray and I saw the right side of his face first, followed by the left side. He had a gray mustache and beard and had very piercing eyes.

On the evening of October 6, 2010, I was privileged to see the face of God again. I had prayed for several days prior to seeing God's face and was very delighted that God appeared before me once again.

Before I saw the face of God, I saw to my immediate left a pink arm of an angel. I didn't know the significance of the pink arm but immediately after I saw the pink arm, I saw the face of God to my immediate right. God's face was in color this time with the same mustache and beard. However, this time, God seemed very warm to me with the feeling of love.

Of course, God is love and He wants everyone to love Him at all times and to pray to Him as well. I do pray to God and love Him very much as well and pray to Him many times every day during my entire life. The pink arm of the angel appeared for only a few seconds and God's face appeared for only a few seconds as well. God was white and appeared to be in his 50's with a rustic face, brown hair, brown mustache and brown beard. He is very handsome and, of course, has an air of confidence as he should have, of course.

In May 2011, I was praying to God as I always do during the evening. I soon fell asleep but during the night I opened my eyes and saw an arm of an angel above me. The arm was pink with a pink brocade covering. The arm appeared for only a few seconds and disappeared quickly.

The very next day, I saw the same pink arm with the pink brocade covering and it disappeared quickly as before. I soon realized that this was the same arm that appeared prior to the appearance of God's face and the arm belonged to my guardian angel.

A few days later, I saw a large pink flower-like appearance at the upper left part of my bedroom ceiling. The appearance lasted for only a few seconds and seemed to be rotating inward before it disappeared. The flower was about one foot in diameter and it was very beautiful and relaxing as well.

Again, after a few days, during the middle of the night, I saw the cherub that appeared just after the birth of our two children, Jasmine and Jessica. Only this time, the cherub was in black and white and appeared multiple times on the wall beside me.

I was lying on my right side, my most comfortable position, and my left eye was open but my right eye was buried in the pillow. I saw my cherub with my left eye as he appeared on the wall in numerous ways before he disappeared after two to four seconds. I was very happy to see my cherub since I had been praying many times to see him again.

When we visited the Philippines previously during a New Year's Eve celebration. I stayed with Jasmine and Jessica at our condominium in Manila since they were very young, perhaps two or three years old. Traditionally, in the Philippines, New Year's is celebrated with lighting fireworks.

I heard all of the fireworks going off outside but Jasmine and Jessica were sound asleep. Suddenly, I saw their cherub between both girls, giggling and moving around between them very happily. He was about their size but a small boy now, the same size as he was in my home against the wall. The girl's cherub has grown up now but is still taking care of Jasmine and Jessica much as the same as my guardian Angel is taking care of me.

I prayed for several days to see my guardian angel. Finally, I did see her when she came towards me at a very fast speed, first the left side of her face and then the right side of her face. She was very pretty but was visible in tones of gray only. She appeared for only a few seconds before disappearing.

In June 2011, I was praying to God to help and protect my family. My business was very slow and I needed God's help to pay my bills and take care of my family. During the middle of the night, a man's arm appeared with a large green ring on his finger. I believed that this was a sign from God that I would receive a down payment from a client.

The very next day, I did receive a large down payment from a client and gave thanks to God for his divine intervention. I could not survive without God's support. God has been supporting and protecting me and my family all of my life and I am very thankful and pray to Him every day and always will love Him and obey Him as well!

On August 21, 2011, I received a phone call from my son, David, that his mother, my ex-wife, was killed in a car accident in Georgia. Needless to say, everyone was devastated from the bad news. David, Elizabeth and Susan, my three children from my first marriage, were all in shock and needed immediate comforting. It was a real tragedy and no one expected such a terrible happening.

I flew to San Francisco and met David and Susan along with the Korean relatives and went to a memorial service. When I got back, I was feeling the sorrow as were my three children. I prayed to God to be comforted as well.

A few days later, during the early morning hours, I saw an arm appear above me with the hand down in a comforting gesture. The arm appeared for only a second but I knew that it was God who was comforting me.

I was very scared at the time since the arm appeared at once and disappeared quickly. I didn't expect such a miracle to appear so soon after my prayers but later was very happy to have been comforted by God in such a manner.

A few days later, an arm appeared beside me and was outstretched on my right side. This was also God's comforting me after the serious tragedy of my ex-wife's death.

In September 2011, I was praying to see my guardian angel. During the middle of the night, I did see my guardian angel for a few seconds on the left corner of my room. She was standing up and appeared to be about five feet tall. She was gray in color and had very long wings behind her back, stretching all the way past her knees to her ankles.

A few weeks later, I was praying again to see my guardian angel in color. Several days afterwards, during the middle of the night, I did see her face in color for a few seconds. She was very beautiful and very young, appearing to be in her early 20's and was Asian. I felt very blessed to have actually seen my guardian angel in color, just the same as I saw God's very handsome face in color as well.

One of my clients was feeling very sad and needed immediate comforting. I told her about my guardian angel and that I would ask her to visit her to make her feel better. My client went outside to the back of her townhouse on the upper deck a few days later and looked up into the sky. Suddenly, she saw my guardian angel and described her perfectly as being Asian with slanted eyes and her wings behind her back down to her ankles.

She saw my guardian angel in tones of gray and was simply delighted at seeing her and felt immediately comforted. I was very delighted that my guardian angel actually visited my client and I thanked her for her holy visitation.

In the spring of 2015, I felt that someone was looking at me. I opened my eyes and to my immediate right I saw a very small, beautiful angel with small wings at a 45 degree angle. She was no more than 12" tall and was simply adorable! She was leaning against my laundry stand in my bedroom about 18" above the floor. The angel was in color and was white. I have never seen such a wonderful sight and was simply amazed! She has never appeared to me again.

Several years ago, I saw several hundred angels at one time in the upper right corner of my ceiling. These angels resembled large mosquitoes to me since they were so small. All of a sudden, one of the angels fell down from the group but I don't know where it landed. All of the angels were black in color and I knew they were angels since they all had very tiny, thin wings.

At about the same time, we had a very bad weather system known as a derecho which passed through our area. We heard a loud noise behind our house and our lawn and house was strewn with pieces of trees and limbs everywhere.

When I looked at the backyard, I saw a large tree in my neighbor's back yard with damage to our chain link fence which we shared jointly. I soon discovered that the tree was from my back yard and it was yanked up from our yard and placed in my neighbor's yard in the entire length from the back of his house to the back fence.

Luckily, there was no damage to my neighbor's house. I felt that God had intervened to protect my family from harm since the tree which measured about 50 feet long and two feet in diameter was deposited in my neighbor's yard instead of crashing down on my own home. This was truly a miracle! I immediately prayed to God, thanking Him for preventing injury to my family and home.

We had a power outage due to the derecho and went down to the basement due to the lack of electricity and air conditioning. We all slept in the same room since it was much cooler than upstairs.

When I was praying in the evening, I saw the same group of tiny, mosquito like angels in the upper right corner of the ceiling. They were so tiny with tiny wings and I immediately recognized them. It felt very comforting to be with such a large group of angels and I felt privileged to be with them once again.

I don't really know why God and His angels have chosen me to reveal themselves. I feel blessed, however, to know that God is in fact real and alive and His angels are real and alive as well.

During all of my life, I have witnessed numerous sightings of God, His angels, and one of His cherubs in my home. The sightings have normally occurred prior to an important occasion such as the death of a loved one or the birth of our babies.

Most of the sightings have been in color but some of them have been in tones of gray. God has encouraged me to write this book in the many ways which I have described.

I feel that the main reason why God and his angels have appeared before me is to reassure everyone that God does in fact exist and that he has an army of angels to do his work.

I know for a fact that God and His angels can read my mind and know exactly what I am thinking at the time I am thinking about something. All through my life, God has been protecting my family and me from harms' way. He knows the future, of course, and has been guiding humanity since the beginning of time. God created life in all of its many forms on our planet and perhaps even on other planets that we have yet to discover.

I hope that anyone reading this book will come to appreciate the role which God and His angels have played since the beginning of time. I also hope that anyone reading this book will continue to believe in God and His angels as having an active role in our lives forever.

On May 14, 2015, I needed to wake up at 6:15 a.m. I was still sleeping when I heard a small boy's voice, "Wake up daddy!" This was the only time I heard my twins' cherub's voice. The voice was clearly a small boy's voice and I was very happy to hear the cherub's voice. The voice was a little husky and I knew immediately that the voice belonged to my twins' cherub.

On May 18, 2015, I had to get up at 6:15 a.m. as well. Suddenly, there was a tapping on my pillow at exactly 6:15 a.m. I knew immediately that my guardian angel tapped on my pillow to wake me up and was very happy that she has continued to take care of me at all times.

During the week of September 21, 2015, Pope Francis arrived in the United States for his first papal visit here. He was greeted at the Joint Base Andrews at Prince Georges County, Maryland by President Obama and the First Lady.

Pope Francis spent the entire week here in Washington, D.C. beginning with a White House welcoming ceremony with President Obama, a midday prayer with U.S. Bishops at Saint Matthews Cathedral, a Junipero Serra Canonization Mass at the Basilica of the National Shrine of the Immaculate Conception, a speech before a joint session of Congress and a visit to St. Patrick's Catholic Church and Catholic Charities of the Archdiocese of Washington. He was due to travel to New York and Philadelphia for additional activities as well.

Pope Francis is a very humble and gracious individual. I watched him speaking and interacting before numerous different walks of life and he is very sincere and warm. I especially enjoyed his asking many individuals to pray for him, something that shows his true holy stature in the Catholic Church. He deeply cares for all individuals and asks us to follow the golden rule of treating others as we would like others to treat ourselves. I also enjoyed his saying, "God bless America", before the U.S. Congress.

I was watching one of my favorite TV shows the other day, the Discovery Channel. I love to watch all of their animal shows, especially the shows about sharks. The show stated that sharks have been on our planet for 400 million years. If this is true, this proves that God has been with us since the beginning of time since he created the heaven and earth along with all living creatures, including man, not to mention sharks, dinosaurs and everything else.

This gives us great pause to wonder how God and his angels have been with us since the beginning of time and where they came from. I know that this may not be a good question to ask but I think about where our solar system came from as well and how many solar systems exist in space. I also think about whether our solar system has a beginning and ending and about the possibility of life on other planets. Only God and his angels know the answers to these questions.

Albert Einstein developed the formula E=mc(squared) in other words, energy equals mass times the square of the speed of light. With this concept, in theory, when man travels in space, time stands still.

His Special Theory of Relativity has just been confirmed in that magnetic waves permeate throughout the solar system which affect all planets in our solar system. Confirmation was made in the spring of 2016. It took 100 years from his Special Theory of Relativity to be confirmed by scientists.

In November 2015, we visited our relatives in Los Angeles. It was a very restful trip to be with our relatives and to enjoy Thanksgiving as well. I baked my famous "low calorie" pecan pies and brownies which were enjoyed by everyone.

During one of the mornings, I was walking down from the upstairs alone when I heard a voice saying, "Good morning John!" The voice was a woman's voice and it was very loud. I quickly replied, "Good morning!" as well and looked around but didn't see anyone in the area. I then realized that the voice came from my guardian angel. The voice was clearly from an Asian woman since I recognized the accent.

This is only the second time that I have heard her voice since the time that she had whispered the word, "God", in my left ear when God's spirit rose from my body prior to my father's death in 1999. Hearing my guardian angel's voice was truly a miracle and I will never forget it! Her voice was truly sweet and beautiful and I was really amazed and taken aback at hearing her speaking to me. No one in my relative's family ever calls me by my first name and I knew that my guardian Angel, Divine, had greeted me that morning!

It is now the summer of 2016. I am comforted by the constant presence of my guardian angel, Divine, since she lets me know that she is around me by tapping on the walls, tapping on the living room television, and tapping on the numerous bottles of water in the first floor of our house.

Even when I am driving my car she taps on my water bottle in my arm rest when I am sometimes drowsy to keep me awake to avoid having an accident. I feel very blessed to have my own guardian angel to take care of me at all times!

In the middle of August of 2016, I received a phone call from my brother's landlord stating that he was in the hospital since he had fallen in his apartment. The landlord stated that my brother, Richard E.

Seiden, I called him, "Dickie," had apparently fallen down on his left side and lay alone for three days.

It was very hard to fathom how anyone could survive laying alone for three days without food or water! I called Holy Cross Hospital in Silver Spring since it was the closest to his apartment in Silver Spring to see if he was taken there. I leaned that he was taken to the emergency room where he was being treated.

Josie and I immediately visited him in the Emergency Room of the hospital. Dickie looked extremely frail and had both an oxygen and feeding tube attached to him for life support. He could not talk but instead barely lifted his head to acknowledge our presence. He had a gash on the left side of his head since he had fallen on some object which caused an indentation.

Since my brother was on life support, I spoke with his doctor about his chances for survival. The doctor stated that perhaps he should be placed in a group home since he could not take care of himself.

Dickie has had numerous caregivers to take care of him over the years and I didn't understand why he did not have the caregiver with him when he fell down in his apartment all alone. I immediately began to think about where I could place him in a group home since I had placed my mother in a group home five years ago and she is doing just fine with excellent care by the group home's staff.

Dickie and I have had numerous phone conversations while he was in the hospital and always ended the conversation with, "I love you," at the end of the phone call.

After a week, I visited him alone during the weekend prior to our birthday, August 29th. We both had the same birthday with two years apart; Dickie was two years older than me. My mother was always asked during the years how we happened to have been born on the same day, two years apart. Her answer was always, "Good planning!"

Dickie continued to be very frail and was off the oxygen tube and feeding tube so I thought that he was recovering. In fact, he had refused the feeding tube according to his doctor since he had told his doctor that he wanted to die either in the hospital or at home. I didn't know this fact until later.

On our joint birthday, we had numerous conversations in which we greeted each other with, "happy birthday!" Dickie even added, "I love you, man!" and I replied, "I love you, too!"

Later in our conversation, Dickie again stated, "I love you, too!" and I replied, "I love you three!" He laughed at my humor since I always joke around, especially in trying circumstances!

On August 30, 2016, I received a phone call from my brother's doctor stating that my brother had died that morning. Since Dickie had refused the feeding tube, his body had simply shut down. It was simply devastating! I had expected to place him in a group home with 24 hour care but this plan was now out of the question. My brother had chosen to die!

I had the unpleasant task of telling my mother of Dickie's passing. She was devastated as well! It is still impacting on my mother since every time I visit her at her group home she is still grieving at his loss.

Fortunately, I had a framed photograph of my mother with Dickie which I brought her after his death to comfort her. She was very pleased to receive the photograph to remind her of their love.

Almost every evening I get up in the middle of the night to use the bathroom. The night is very dark and I never need to use a light because I am accustomed to the darkness.

From time to time, however, a bright light appears at the window for a fraction of a second. The bright light repeats itself a few seconds later and stops. This has been going on for a number of months now and I feel that it is a sign from God, showing me His love.

During the time that I am waiting for Jasmine and Jessica to come out of their school to be picked up, I also saw a bright light at the top level of the school when I was looking in its direction. This was also a sign from God since the light lasted only a fraction of a second as well. I always feel very comforted that God is watching over me with these signs from Him.

When we had the derecho hit our home several years ago, we had slept in the basement due to the power outage and a lack of air conditioning. The basement was much cooler than the floors above and we were able to sleep. During the evening, I noticed a large amount of angels that appeared like mosquitoes with wings. Each angle was a fraction of an inch long and had very tiny wings.

From time to time, I have noticed a single one of these very tiny angels flying around me when I am in the upstairs kitchen. I know that it's not a mosquito since mosquitoes are not around in the winter.

One time, thinking that the angel was a mosquito, I tried to catch it. However, the angel was too fast and I was not able to catch it. Later, I thought that I was wrong to have tried to catch it since it was really not a mosquito after all!

I have not heard from my daughter, Elizabeth for six months now. The date is February 5, 2017, and the last I had any contact from her was in July of 2016 when she sent me a birthday card and present.

Since my birthday was in August, I was puzzled why she had sent me the present and card so early. I called my other daughter, Susan, and asked her to try and locate Elizabeth since she had talked with Elizabeth's friend, Roger, from time to time. However, Susan was not able to locate Elizabeth for a number of months even after talking to Roger.

Luckily, I had Roger's phone number which Susan had given to me. Last week I was finally able to speak with Roger. He said that he was very concerned about Elizabeth as I was and was wondering if she were still alive. Fortunately, Roger said that Elizabeth finally had called her a few days prior to my phone call with him to say that she is still in Dallas, Texas.

We were both relieved that she was still alive! Without contact for such a long time, we were both worried about her safety and welfare as were Susan and David. I always feel that it is very important to maintain contact with the family at all times!

During the past six months when I had no contact with Elizabeth, I constantly prayed to God and asked Him if Elizabeth is okay. God always answered me that she was just fine and not to worry. I must have asked God over 100 times in my prayer to Him about Elizabeth's welfare and He always responded that she was just fine and not to worry.

After speaking with Roger, I was greatly relieved about Elizabeth's contact with him and was so thankful for God's reassurance that she was just fine. God always replied, "She is just fine; doing her thing." I didn't question what "doing her thing" meant since I just wanted to know that she was okay. With God's reassurance that Elizabeth was okay these many months, I was always comforted. God is always with us and always takes care of us as well!

From time to time, I will be sitting on my easy chair in the living room when I will see a flashing light across the street in front of a neighbor's house. The light will flash several times and then stop flashing. This has happened numerous times. The light flashing will also occur behind my house in front of another house as seen through my bathroom window.

All of these light flashings occur during the evening and appear generally on a random basis. I know now that they are signs from God and serve to let me know of His presence. I know that God is always with me and appreciate his presence at all times!

During the night, I always wake up several times to go to the bathroom. Often, during the darkness, a light will appear through the window lighting up the bathroom for several seconds. This has been happening for the past year from 2016 up to the present, March 11, 2017.

I know that this is a sign from God to give me comfort. I pray to God, my guardian angel whom I call Divine, all of the other angels and my daughters' cherub every day for numerous times; even during the nighttime. I call all of them my holy family and always enjoy their presence.

On February 16th, I lay awake during the night when a large face of God appeared on my ceiling. His face was about three feet wide and six feet long. I have never seen God's face so large before but was immediately comforted at His holy presence.

The very next day I saw my guardian angel, Divine's face during the evening as well. She was so beautiful and was smiling at me at a very sharp angle with her chin resting on her hand. I was very happy to be visited by God and my guardian angel just one day apart.

During the morning of March 11th, at 7:00 a.m. there were a series of tappings on my front door. First, five taps, then silence; then five more taps, then silence; finally, five more taps, then silence.

I immediately ran to the front door expecting to see someone standing there. To my surprise, there was no one at the front door. Josie told me that there should not be anyone there at this time.

I was really shocked to hear what appeared to be human fingers tapping at the front door. My guardian angel has been tapping numerous times over the years on water bottles in my room, on the television, on the walls, and on many other items and locations throughout the house. This is the first time, however, that she has tapped on the front door.

At precisely one hour later, at 8:00 a.m., she tapped once again with exactly the same scenario; five taps then silence; five more taps then silence; and finally, five more taps and then silence. I immediately ran to the front door and opened it once more to find no one outside.

This was really scary but I know that Divine likes to make her presence known to me. I do really appreciate her holy presence whenever she decides to make herself known to me. But this morning's tapping were really unnerving, to say the least.

Josie didn't think anything of the tapping but she does not believe in my guardian angel. I have had so much contact with Divine over the years that I immediately recognize the various forms of contact that she provides for her recognition. I really enjoy interacting with Divine since she is with God's holy family.

We have had the warmest winter on record in 2016 to 2017. Many days have been in the high 60's and even low 70's. I have been praying to God for warm weather during the winter and He has responded with simply beautiful weather. I have called this beautiful weather, "Winter-Spring," since it has been like spring during the past three months.

Next week, however, the weather men are forecasting our first possible snow storm for Tuesday, March 14th. I have been praying to God to have this potential snowfall miss the Washington, D.C. area since heavy snows are always to disruptive. Well, we shall see what happens next week!

On March 8th, I was in the bathroom in the middle of the night as usual when a bright light entered the room. I looked out of the bathroom window and saw a beautiful full moon above. The moon was very bright and simply beautiful!

I know that God has made heaven and earth along with the entire universe and I really appreciated the moon's presence that evening. It was like a miracle to see the beautiful, bright moon during the evening when all was quiet!

Well, we had our big 1 ½ inch snow fall in the middle of March. God has answered my prayers for a minimal amount of snow this year. Last year we had several feet of snow with drifts up to four feet.

I believe in global warming since the earth is gradually getting warmer. This is especially noticeable in the Artic and Antarctica where the ice is melting very quickly over the years, depriving such wildlife as polar bears from food sources and maintenance of their habitat.

This morning was April 1st. Normally, in the morning I take my assortment of medicine including my vitamins and cholesterol medication as well. When I was reaching for my cholesterol pill in my pill box, one of the pills was shaking by itself. The shaking reminded me of the small plant that my guardian angel, Divine, shook beneath my back porch a few years ago to get my attention.

Pills just cannot shake themselves! This was an obvious sign from Divine that she is always with me. I was really surprised to see a pill shaking in this manner. It was like a rock and roll move from the 50's called the, "twist"!

My family will be travelling to Los Angeles on April 5th for an eleven day trip and to return on Easter Sunday, April 16th back to Maryland on an overnight trip. Josie hasn't seen her parents in 1 ½ years and is very anxious to see her parents along with her brothers and sisters as well. Jasmine, Jessica and I are also very anxious to see everyone. This will be a nice vacation for all of us during the girls' spring break.

Luckily, I was able to obtain nonstop tickets on two airlines, United Airlines from Baltimore to Los Angeles and Alaska Airlines from Los Angeles back to Baltimore. We have been travelling as a family ever since Jasmine and Jessica were born nine years ago. Our trips have included the Philippines, Hong Kong, Singapore, New York and, of course, Los Angeles. Josie and Justin and I went to Hawaii before the girls were born and we hope to return to Hawaii to let them experience the beautiful state.

Hopefully, we can go to Europe this summer since this is one place that Josie and the girls have not visited. I have had the privilege of visiting many countries in Europe including Germany, France, England, Belgium, and Holland. I look forward to a trip to Europe once again to be with my family and to be able to practice my German and French languages.

Normally, as the saying goes, "If you don't use a language, you lose it!" This is very true and I look forward to regaining some of my lost French and German when we visit both countries in addition to England. I would love to visit Italy since I love Italian food! We will have to see what shall transpire.

Josie mentioned to me that her relatives and friends in California are planning a European trip this summer and we may join them. It may all depend on the travel plans for everyone to be sure that we all agree on the itinerary!

My mother will be turning 97 years old on April 18th. She has been living in a group home for seven years now and has been receiving excellent care. I bring her supplies from time to time such as diapers, Ensure vitamin drinks, wipes and other items she needs from time to time.

I just brought her a new pair of shoes which she asked me to purchase for her. The first pair was too small at size 6. However, the second pair which was a size 7 ½ with a fur lining fit just right. Since she always wears very thick socks, I decided to purchase a larger size. Her shoe size is normally 5 ½ but due to her wide feet and thick socks, I decided to take a chance on a larger size!

I just ordered a very nice cake from Costco today which will be ready when we come back from California. The cake has yellow roses on the top, her favorite flower, and has a white buttercream frosting on the top with a white cheese cake filling. I am sure that this delicious, "low calorie" cake will be enjoyed by one and all!

I have been baking brownies, chocolate chip cookies, cheese cakes, regular cakes, pecan pies and other, "low calorie" desserts for over 50 years now. My specialty is brownies which I add chocolate chips and walnuts for extra flavor and taste. I even brought in my baked goods to my former U.S. government office to celebrate special events with my co-workers. Everyone always enjoyed my "low calorie" baked desserts, of course. I even bring my brownies to my mother's group home from time to time and they are normally gone within an hour. I am always happy to bring my brownies to her group home since everyone, including the staff, enjoys them immensely!

We traveled to Los Angeles on April 5, 2017, with a non-stop flight with United Airlines. I usually sit on an aisle seat with my left arm on the armrest. During the flight, someone stroked my left arm five times with each stroke stronger and stronger. Since my guardian angel has stroked my left arm during previous flights, I immediately knew that it was her again.

I looked in front of me and behind me on the aisle but there was no one in the area at all. Divine was giving me a message that she was always with me, no matter whether I was on the ground or in the air!

The flight was smooth and, after landing, we took a bus to another location nearby for our car rental. Luckily, we were able to rent a large SUV with plenty of room for my family plus other members of Josie's family.

Before leaving Maryland, Josie found out that her father was experiencing difficulty breathing. He was brought to a nearby hospital for evaluation which determined that he had heart problems in addition to a tumor in one of his lungs.

The family had a group meeting and decided to focus on the heart problem since the tumor was not of an emergency basis. Eventually, her father was placed into surgery to have a heart pacemaker installed in his chest. The operation was successful and he was returned home afterwards.

The following week, he had a checkup with a cardiac doctor and was deemed to be in good health. Her father is 89 years old and underweight so he has to be monitored closely at all times.

While we were staying at my sister-in-law's home in Santa Clarita, California, during the morning of April 12th, I was walking down the upstairs hallway when I hear my name called, "John, John", in a subdued woman's voice. I distinctly recognized the voice as that of my guardian angel, Divine.

The time was about 5:00 a.m. and everyone was asleep. I know that she wanted to greet me and to let me know that she is always with me and truly appreciated her greeting. I know that she spoke to me in a subdued voice since she didn't want to wake up anybody.

While visiting Josie's father in the hospital on a daily basis, we had to drive on the numerous freeways in Los Angeles. Josie drove during the day and I drove at night. Driving in Los Angeles is extremely complicated and dangerous since everyone drives at a very high speed and quite often, in a reckless manner. Fortunately, we were able to survive driving in Los Angeles for the eleven days we stayed in the state.

Josie hadn't seen her family for one and one-half years so she was very happy to see them again. Jasmine and Jessica hadn't seen their close friend, Kaythe, as well and had a good time during the trip.

As a matter of fact, Jasmine and Jessica went to Disneyland and Universal Studios once again and thoroughly enjoyed themselves with all of the rides and food at the amusement parks. They especially enjoyed the rollercoaster rides since they travel so fast!

During our trip back to Baltimore aboard Alaska Airlines, once again my guardian angel, Divine, made her presence known. This time, she tapped my right wrist five times to make her presence known. I was really surprised to have this form of contact since she usually brushes against my left arm.

My mother's birthday was on April 18th when she turned 97 years old. I brought the cake which I ordered from Costco to her group home with Josie, Jasmine, Jessica and myself to enjoy her birthday celebration along with all members of the group home and the staff as well. Everyone enjoyed the, "low calorie", cake and my mother blew out the candles.

I have been asking Divine to wake me up prior to 6:30 a.m. every day since I have to get up to check my emails and place calls overseas for my international consulting business on a regular basis. Normally, Divine will make a tapping sound on the walls in my bedroom to wake me up.

However, on April 26th, she tapped on my lips very gently for five times. This immediately woke me up and I was presently surprised with this new maneuver. There must be something special about her tapping me on my lips or on my hand for five times. There must also be something special about her brushing against my left arm for five times as well as tapping on the front screen door for five times. I don't know whether this pattern is significant or just her habit. Anyway, I appreciate very much her very kind and thoughtful attention to me since she is my guardian angel and is in God's holy family!

Today is June 9th and I always pick up Jasmine and Jessica after school and walk them home. Since the weather was in the low 80's and was a sunny and beautiful day, I let the girls play in their school playground for 15 minutes outside. Both girls bring a bottle of water to school every day to drink after recess and during the school day.

I normally sit on an adjacent park bench and wait for the girls to finish their playing. Today, however, there seas a popping sound in Jessica's backpack which sounded like her water bottle making a noise. The popping sound occurred four more times with the last popping sound somewhat muted. I knew that my guardian angel, Divine, had made the sounds to let me know of her presence once again. The routine of five sounds was simply reminiscent of Divine's habit in letting me know that she is with me at all times and I truly appreciated her devotion to me!

Today was September 19. My brother, Dickie, had passed away on August 30, 2016, over one year now. Suddenly, in the middle of the night, his face appeared to me in color between myself and the ceiling. I was so surprised to see him, especially in the middle of the night. He looked so young and handsome, appearing to be about 25 to 30 years old. Dickie had a very nice smile and his face was at a 45-degree angle to the ceiling. His face appeared for only a few seconds, but I was very happy to see him again, especially since he is in heaven. Dickie appeared to be very happy, so I know that God is taking care of him at all times!

I truly hope that anyone reading this book will appreciate the fact that God and His angels are real and are with us at all times. I pray to God and His holy family each and every day and know that one day I will be joining them in heaven. However, while I am here on Earth, I will be trying to take care of my own family the best as I can for their health and welfare and a successful future. I always pray for God and His angels' divine guidance and protection, especially during these troubling times with numerous international conflicts occurring every day. Perhaps one day people will realize that we must in fact love one another instead of fighting for control of land and property. Time will tell!

ANDROMEDA
NASA S63-271

GODDARD MISSIONS
ARIEL
VANGUARD I
PIONEER V–EXPLORER V
S-15
P-21
VANGUARD III
OSO
NERV
EXPLORER VIII
P-14
EXPLORER X
EXPLORER VII
S-3
EXPLORER XII
ECHO
TIROS I, II, III, IV, V

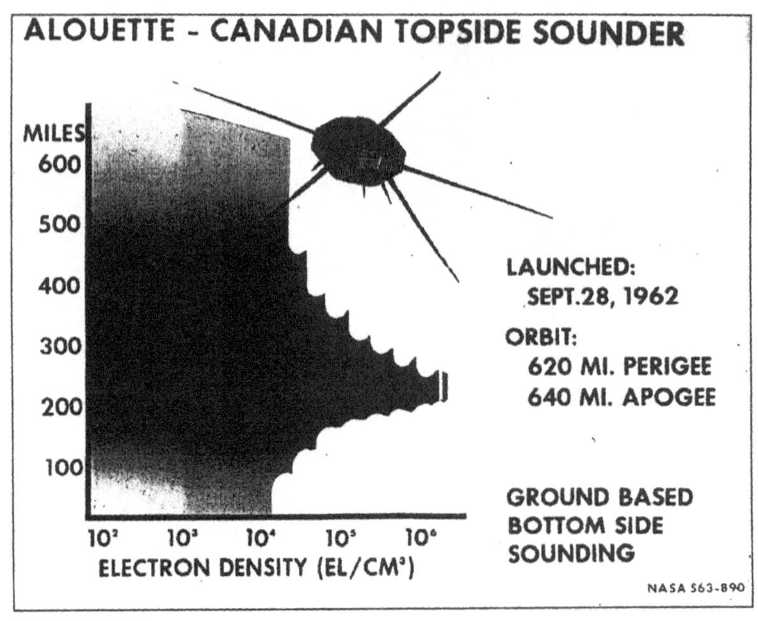
ALOUETTE - CANADIAN TOPSIDE SOUNDER
MILES
600
500
400
300
200
100
ELECTRON DENSITY (EL/CM³)
LAUNCHED:
SEPT. 28, 1962
ORBIT:
620 MI. PERIGEE
640 MI. APOGEE
GROUND BASED
BOTTOM SIDE
SOUNDING
NASA S63-890

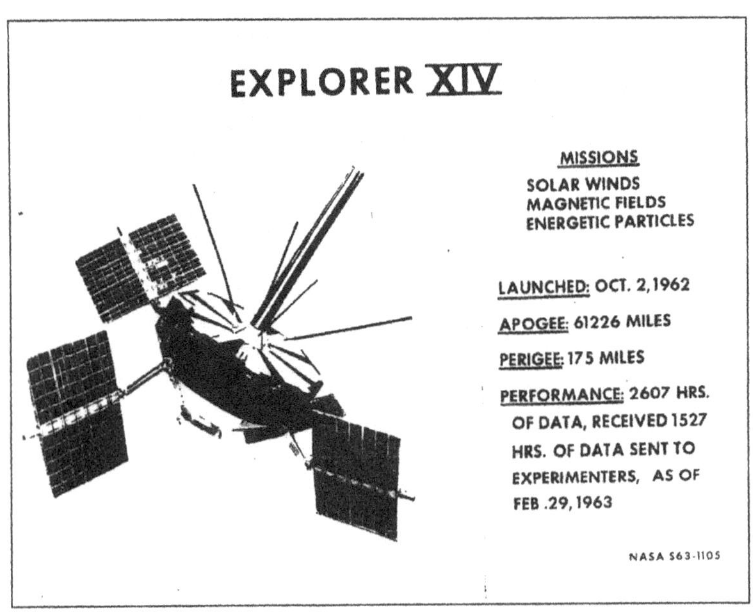
EXPLORER XIV
MISSIONS
SOLAR WINDS
MAGNETIC FIELDS
ENERGETIC PARTICLES
LAUNCHED: OCT. 2, 1962
APOGEE: 61226 MILES
PERIGEE: 175 MILES
PERFORMANCE: 2607 HRS.
OF DATA, RECEIVED 1527
HRS. OF DATA SENT TO
EXPERIMENTERS, AS OF
FEB. 29, 1963
NASA S63-1105

WILLIAM DONALD SCHAEFER, Mayor
OFFICE OF THE MAYOR · CITY OF BALTIMORE
7th Floor, 131 East Redwood Street, Baltimore, Maryland 21202 (301) 396-3100

In reply refer to:

MO-4

May 28, 1976

Mr. John J. Seiden
11507 Amhelst Avenue
Apartment 3
Wheaton, Maryland 20902

Dear Mr. Seiden:

I am writing to you to express my
sentiments for your unsuccessful
bid for a Congressional seat in
the Democratic Primary. Your campaign attempt was an admirable one,
and one in which you should take
great pride. Best wishes for the
future.

Sincerely,

Don Schaefer

Mayor

OFFICE OF THE DIRECTOR

UNITED STATES DEPARTMENT OF JUSTICE

FEDERAL BUREAU OF INVESTIGATION

WASHINGTON, D.C. 20535

August 31, 1970

AIRMAIL

Mr. John J. Seiden
Safety Division
Hq., 2nd Inf. Div.
APO San Francisco 96224

Dear Mr. Seiden:

Your letter and Application for Federal Employment were received on August 20, 1970.

I appreciate your interest in this Bureau and, for your information, I am enclosing material concerning our Special Agent position. We presently anticipate no vacancies in this position until June, 1971, or later. However, should you wish to have your qualifications placed on record for consideration when openings do occur, execute and submit the enclosed application to the FBI field office nearest you upon your return to this country. One of my representatives will be available to discuss the matter with you at that time and answer any questions you might have.

Sincerely yours,

John Edgar Hoover
Director

Enclosures (4)